O9-ABF-306

APR 22 2002

Beyond Mayfield

Beyond Mayfield

Vaunda Micheaux Nelson

G. P. Putnam's Sons · New York

RETA E KING LIBRARY
CHADRON STATE COLLEGE
CHADRON, NE 69337

Copyright © 1999 by Vaunda Micheaux Nelson
All rights reserved. This book, or parts thereof, may not be reproduced
in any form without permission in writing from the publisher.
G. P. Putnam's Sons, a division of Penguin Putnam Books for Young Readers,
345 Hudson Street, New York, NY 10014.
G. P. Putnam's Sons, Reg. U.S. Pat. & Tm. Off.
Published simultaneously in Canada.
Printed in the United States of America.
Text set in Palatino.

Library of Congress Cataloging-in-publication Data
Nelson, Vaunda Micheaux.
Beyond Mayfield/Vaunda Micheaux Nelson. p. cm.
Summary: In 1961 the children of Mayfield are concerned with
air-raid drills and fallout shelters, but the civil rights movement
becomes real when a neighbor joins the Freedom Riders.
[1. Afro-Americans—Fiction.   2. Race relations—Fiction.
3. Civil rights workers—Fiction.   4. Schools—Fiction.
5. Fallout shelters—Fiction.   6. Recluses—Fiction.]
I. Title.   PZ7.N4377Maye   1999   [Fic]—dc21   98-35692   CIP   AC
ISBN 0-399-23355-5
10 9 8 7 6 5 4 3 2

PELLE C. KIMBLE LIBRARY
CASTELOON STATE COLLEGE
GRAUGHAM, ME 06037

N3386

11⁷⁰

Midwest

4-4-02

For my brothers and sisters,
Eddie, Neé, Gina, and Billie

and for Refna

Prologue

Mama once said you have to give people a chance even if they don't always treat you right. She said sometimes they're just afraid.

I thought about that and later asked, "Why would people be scared of me?"

"It isn't just you," Papa said. "We're all fearful of what isn't like us, of what we don't understand."

"Like flying saucers?"

"Yes," Mama said, brushing back my bangs with her hand. "But also people like . . ." She paused and raised an eyebrow. " . . . Mr. Slater."

I looked at the floor and tugged my pigtail. Even though I knew better, I had to admit I was still a little bit scared of Old Hairy Slater.

But Old Hairy was the least of my worries. Since our old school had closed and we started going to the new one at

Parkview, I'd been learning a few things. Things that living in Mayfield Crossing had made me dumb about. And when Dillon Wood's brother, Lucky, came home from the Navy, I found out I wasn't the only one.

Lucky came back a month after President Kennedy moved into the White House, and the next day, everybody in Mayfield celebrated. Mr. Wood had a backyard barbeque, even though it was the middle of February and freezing outside. Dillon was so proud he kept saying, "Lucky, tell them about the submarine," or "Lucky, tell them about the sharks," stories he'd heard just the night before but wanted us to hear, too. We ate inside and sat around the Woods' living room listening to Lucky tell stories. None of us knew then how soon he would leave Mayfield again. And none of us could have guessed what his leaving would mean.

Chapter 1

I rolled over and opened my eyes. Why was it so light? I jumped out of bed and ran down the hall. "Mama, you forgot to wake us for school!"

"No, I didn't, Meg," she said. "There's no school today."

"Why not?" I couldn't believe it. Had God heard my prayer the night before?

Mama motioned me to come to the living room window. I walked over and she put her arm around me. Then she pushed back the curtains.

"Wow!" was all I could say.

"It snowed a little," Mama said, pushing my mouth closed.

A *little*? It was everywhere, piled on the trees and the road, and our car looked just like a big white mountain. The wind had drifted snow almost up to the windowsill, and it was still falling. I could see Papa outside shoveling the walk. He hadn't gone to work.

3

I looked at Mama. "Is it the good kind?" She knew what I meant. If the snow was too dry, it wouldn't stick together and you couldn't make snowballs.

Mama opened the window and pushed some snow into her hand. It held together in a nice little ball. "Looks good to me," she said, just before a snowball flew in the window. Papa!

Mama laughed, but pretended to be mad.

I ran back to the bedroom and jumped on my brother's bed.

"Billie!"

"Hey! What are you doin'? Get off, Meg!"

I stood over him and shouted, "Snow day!"

The mad look left Billie's face. "Really?" He leaped out of bed and ran to the window, his deep brown eyes even bigger than usual.

"Wow!"

I laughed. "That's what *I* said."

We stood there staring at the whiteness.

"It's the good kind," I told him.

"Great," Billie said. "We can build a fort."

In the bathroom I brushed my teeth and grinned at myself in the mirror. I felt like jumping clean to the sky, like it was my birthday. But I felt a little bit creepy, too, to have a prayer answered so fast.

I couldn't wait to get out in the snow with my best friend Mo Cleary and the rest of the Mayfield gang. But I'd have been just as happy if measles had kept me from school. Not from school so much as from Mrs. Davis. I liked school. But since Mrs. Davis had come, things hadn't felt right. Our regular teacher, Mr. Stanley, had had an operation, and it would take him a while to get better. Mrs. Davis had said he might not come back all year.

I washed my face, dried it with a towel, and groaned at myself in the mirror. Instead of praying that I didn't have to go to school, I should have prayed that Mr. Stanley would get better. Today was a snow day, and maybe even tomorrow, but eventually I'd have to go back to Parkview School and Mrs. Davis. *Shoot!* I'd wasted a prayer, and I was sure that answered ones couldn't be traded for something else.

"Are you making the soap in there, Meg?" Billie yelled from the hall.

I opened the door, ready to defend myself, but Billie was smiling. He wasn't going to let anything spoil the day, and I decided to do the same.

Chapter 2

Just as we were starting breakfast, Mama answered a knock at the door. It was Mo Cleary and her sister, Alice, asking when we were coming out. Mo waved at me, her cheeks pinker than usual. I looked at Mama. "Can we—?"

"Now, Meg," she said, holding the door open. "With this cold weather you especially need your breakfast today."

Mama never let us skip breakfast. Sometimes I wondered what she'd do if there was an air raid first thing in the morning. Would she say, "Finish your oatmeal. You'll need your energy, especially after the explosion"?

Mama turned to Mo and Alice. "They'll be out soon."

"Thank you, Mrs. Turner," they said.

"Have you girls had breakfast yourselves?"

"Yes, ma'am."

Papa took my spoon, scooped up some Cream of Wheat, and shoved it in my mouth. "Eat," he said. So I ate.

After breakfast we put on our snow armor. That's what Billie calls it. By the time we dressed in long underwear, two pairs of socks, pants, shirts, scarves, hats, gloves, and boots, the whole gang was outside.

They'd already cleared a space for the fort in the field next door where we played baseball, and they had a couple of giant snow bricks set down to start the first wall. Luke Cleary and the twins, Fitch and Owen Sherman, were packing snow in boxes to make more bricks. Mo and Alice were helping Dillon Wood make snowballs for the coming battle.

I stood for a moment and looked. The snow was at least two feet deep. It had stopped coming down, and the sun was reflecting so bright you could have worn sunglasses and still been squinting.

Mo ran over, her red hair poking from under the sides of her hat, and hugged me. "Isn't it great?"

"Yeah," I said. "Let's make snow angels."

We found a spot in the field that was still smooth.

"Hey, whatcha doin'?" Alice yelled.

"Angels," I called back. "Come on!"

Alice came over and the three of us held hands and fell backward. We moved our arms up and down to make wings. The hard part was getting up without ruining the pictures.

"Billie, help us!" I called.

"Aw, man," he said, "we're supposed to be building a

fort." He started walking over, but Lucky Wood stepped in front of me and held out his hand. It was like he'd dropped right out of heaven.

"At your service," he said, pulling me up.

"Hey, Lucky, thanks." He was strong, like Papa.

"Yeah, thanks, Lucky," Mo and Alice said as he helped them, too.

We all stood back and looked at the angels. Perfect.

"Nice," Billie said. "Now let's get back to the fort."

"I'll help," Lucky said. And the five of us started walking toward the others.

Lucky was tall, taller than anybody I knew, but not clumsy or awkward like some people his size. He moved like he was real sure of himself.

When Owen saw us coming with Lucky he said, "There you are, our lucky star." Owen was always rhyming that way when he talked.

"Lucky!" Dillon yelled when he saw his brother and ran over.

Luke and Fitch stopped what they were doing, too, and everybody gathered around saying, "Hi, Lucky." "Hey, Lucky." "How ya doin', Lucky." A stranger would never have guessed that we'd all seen him just the day before.

Lucky was smiling, but he seemed uncomfortable.

"Okay now. Quit fussing," he said. "I'm nobody special."

"You heard the ace, he needs some space," Owen sang.

"Sure, Lucky, sure," Dillon said, directing everyone to back away.

"Dillon," Lucky said, laughing. "Relax."

It got quiet.

Lucky brushed some snow from Dillon's shoulder. "How about we get to building?"

"Yeah," Billie agreed.

We all turned to get back to work.

"One more thing," Lucky said, clearing his throat.

We stopped and faced him.

"I don't use the name Lucky much anymore. How about if you just call me by my real name, Sam?"

Dillon frowned, but said quietly, "Sure, Lucky. I mean, Sam." He looked at us. "Did ya hear that?"

"Yeah."

"Okay."

"Sure."

Everybody worked on the fort after that, except Mo and me. We made more snowballs.

"I wonder why he doesn't like 'Lucky' anymore," I said to Mo.

She shrugged. "Maybe since he's grown up he thinks it sounds too much like a kid. They called my dad Johnny when he was little, but now everybody except Gramma calls him John."

"Yeah, probably," I said. But I couldn't help wondering

9

about it. Mr. Wood told us one time how Sam had gotten his nickname. When he was a baby and started walking, Sam fell down a whole flight of stairs and when he hit bottom bounced up and kept walking. Then when he was six, Sam chased a ball onto the road and was hit by a car. It didn't hit him head-on, just sort of swiped him. He was spun to the ground, but he wasn't hurt. Afterward Mrs. Wood hugged him and said, "Maybe we should have named you Lucky." And the name just stuck.

Their mama died when Dillon was five. Mr. Wood was all Dillon had after Sam left, and they were real close, too. Sam wrote Dillon letters from the Navy, and Dillon would tell us about them, but a letter isn't the same as having breakfast with somebody every morning. I was glad for Dillon, glad that Sam was home, even if we couldn't call him Lucky anymore.

I looked over at Sam. I was in first grade when he'd left, so I didn't remember a whole lot about him. I mainly remembered that he and Frank Sherman, the twins' older brother, were best friends, like me and Mo. And I remembered that they used to tell us scary stories about Old Hairy Slater. I could still hear them telling about the time they went to Old Hairy's cabin and looked in the window.

"There, lying on the table in plain sight, was the sharpest-looking hatchet you ever saw," Frank told us.

Then Sam leaned in real close to us and whispered, "And there was hair and blood all over it."

Old Hairy always had a knapsack on his back and we were sure that hatchet was in there, waiting. And with his bushy whiskers, he looked kind of like a werewolf, which made him even scarier.

Fitch and Owen always thought that Old Hairy had something to do with Frank's death. They were only in second grade at the time, but they remember. One night during a storm, somebody came to their front door. The twins were in bed, and started to get up, but Mrs. Sherman went in and told them to stay put. Fitch had gotten a peek, though. He'd seen Old Hairy standing in their doorway carrying Frank. Both of them were soaked to the skin, and Frank wasn't moving. Fitch said he'd caught a glimpse of Sam, too, standing behind them. Mr. Sherman and Sam took Frank to the hospital, and Mrs. Sherman told the twins that Frank had "met with some trouble." After that Frank caught pneumonia and never got better.

Sam joined the Navy right after Frank died.

I made a snowball and added it to the pile, wondering if Sam knew what really happened to Frank, and if he'd ever tell us.

Chapter 3

It took us hours to finish the fort. We liked to make our walls high and have windows and pointed towers like castles do. We were finishing when Mama called us inside for lunch.

She'd made a big pot of vegetable soup and invited the whole gang—the Clearys, the Shermans, and the Woods—to have some. Mama called everybody's parents, while Papa came out on the porch and brushed the snow off us with the broom. Mama had us leave our boots and coats at the front door.

Even though we hadn't wanted to come in when Mama called, I was glad she'd made us. My feet were wet and they tingled and itched. It felt good to get them warm and dry and put on fresh socks.

When we were all squished around the table, Papa said grace and, for a while, there was nothing but the sound of spoons clanking on bowls and people saying "please" and "thank you" as bread was passed around the table.

"Great soup, Mrs. Turner," Fitch said between mouthfuls.

"You wrote the book on how to cook," Owen agreed.

Mama smiled and served them more. "Thank you, boys. You eat your fill now."

"Well, Lucky, how does it feel to be home?" Papa asked as he passed him some bread.

I turned to Papa and whispered, "He doesn't want to be called Lucky anymore. We're supposed to call him Sam."

I was waiting for Papa to ask why, but he just said, "I guess that's understandable. He's a grown man now."

I figured Mo had been right.

"I'm happy to be home, Mr. Turner. More than I can say."

"I know your father couldn't be more pleased," Papa went on. Then he smiled at Dillon. "And this one hasn't stopped grinning since you got back."

Dillon's face turned red, and it seemed almost like his blond cowlick, that was always sticking straight up, drooped a little from embarrassment.

"We're all glad Sam's back," Mama said, squeezing Dillon's shoulder.

"Sam brought Dillon a new camera," Mo said.

"Yeah," Dillon said, "all the way from Tokyo, Japan!"

Dillon liked to take pictures, mostly of animals. His old Brownie camera still worked, but the one Sam got him had all kinds of special dials with numbers. Sam said the pictures would come out better.

"That was very thoughtful, Sam," Mama said. "I don't think you could have chosen a better gift for Dillon."

Sam nodded and smiled.

"What are you going to do now?" Billie asked, piling grape jelly on his bread. Mama gave him a look and he stopped.

"Yeah," Luke said. His glasses were still steamed up from the shock of going from cold to the warm indoors. "Are you gonna get a job?"

Sam ran his hand through his dark crewcut. "I think I'd like to try college. I'm looking into it maybe for September," he said. "The GI Bill would pay."

"That'd mean you'd be going away again," Alice said.

"Yeah, but not until fall," Dillon said. "We'll still get to play ball this summer, won't we, Lucky? I mean Sam." Everybody said Sam was the best hitter in Mayfield.

Sam hesitated, then said, "We'll see."

"Goodness," Mama said, passing a plate of peanut butter cookies around the table. "The poor boy's hardly had a chance to take a breath and already he's expected to have the rest of his life all planned out."

"It's all right, Mrs. Turner." Sam pushed his chair back

14

from the table. "I do have a question for you all, though." He stood up and looked out the window. "Is that big pile of snowballs just to look at or what?"

Everybody laughed and put their snow armor back on.

It was a wild battle. We didn't make two forts and try to steal the flag from the other fort like some kids. We'd make one really good fort and just have a regular snowball fight. We didn't like our fort to get destroyed in the battle, so we just threw snowballs at each other until they were all gone. Then we could keep playing in the fort for days after, until it melted. There was also a rule that we could only throw snowballs from the supply pile. We couldn't make new ones until the next battle.

"Watch out for the Untouchable Turner!" Mo called as Billie threw his famous slow curveball. Owen ducked the wrong way and the snowball knocked his hat clean off.

I was busy laughing when Alice got me in the back. I grabbed two snowballs and chased her to the hedges by our yard. Alice is pretty fast, but I had her cornered without a snowball.

She got down on her knees and begged, "Go ahead, hit me, just please don't get snow down my neck. I'm freezing." Her teeth were chattering.

Before I could throw, I was bombarded from behind. I spun around to see Luke, Billie, and Dillon all running off.

I ran screaming after them, throwing my snowballs as

hard as I could, but I missed by a mile. They were sixth graders and too quick.

"No fair!" Mo yelled. She came over and brushed the snow off me. "Let's get 'em!" I could always count on Mo.

"They're too fast."

"Maybe Sam'll help," Mo said. "That'd even things up."

But Sam and Owen were already coming over.

"You ladies need some assistance?" Sam asked.

"Uh-oh," I heard Luke say. "They're getting reinforcements. We need ammunition, guys." He headed for the snowball supply.

Sam pulled us into a huddle and opened his jacket a little. It was loaded with snowballs.

"Here's what we'll do," he whispered.

"He's the man with a plan." When Owen talked that way, some people thought he was strange. But Sam grinned and put an arm around him.

"Okay," Sam said. "They'll be thinking we don't have ammo, so they'll surround us. Here." He handed out the snowballs. "Keep these hidden until I say the word. Then we'll turn around and let 'em have it."

I looked around. Billie, Luke, Dillon, Fitch, and Alice had gotten snowballs and were starting to surround us, just like Sam said.

Sam whispered, "Stay in the huddle, but move toward the supply pile like we're trying to get some ammo."

16

We moved sideways in our tight huddle. I held my mouth shut tight to keep from giggling.

Billie and the rest of them came real close to us.

"Okay," Sam whispered, "get ready. Act like we're defenseless."

We huddled closer, and Mo and I screamed as they blasted our backs.

"Now!" Sam yelled, and we turned and slammed them with our snowballs. We caught them just like Sam said.

"Heeey!" they cried.

Everybody started laughing and ran for the supply pile. Then it was a free-for-all until the snowballs were gone. Afterward we lay on the snow panting.

Suddenly a snowball dropped out of nowhere and hit the ground by me and Mo. I sat up. Another one hit Sam on the chest.

"Papa!" I started to say, and looked to find him. But it wasn't Papa.

"It's Old Hairy," Dillon said.

Sure enough, Old Hairy was standing at the edge of the field, wearing at least two coats. I wondered if he was smiling, but with his hat and scarf and all those whiskers, I couldn't tell.

"Take cover!" Luke yelled.

Owen pushed past Alice into the fort. Sam started laughing.

Old Hairy held up his hand, then turned toward the woods.

"It's just old Harry Slater," Sam said, smiling. I slipped my hand into his, and we stood outside the fort, watching. The wind had started blowing and was stinging cold. With snow swirling behind him, Old Hairy looked like a disappearing ghost.

"Is he gone?" Fitch asked as I pulled Sam inside the fort. I nodded.

"I guess he wanted to play with us," Sam said.

"Yeah, him and his hatchet," Alice said. She pretended to chop Luke's head off and we all laughed, but then Sam asked us about school.

Chapter 4

"Dillon told me you've had a hard time with the kids at Parkview."

"Yeah, and the teachers, too," Owen said, brushing snow from his tight, dark curls.

Mo squeezed my hand. I knew she was thinking about Mrs. Davis.

Alice frowned. "They don't like us because we're from Mayfield."

"And it's worse for Meg and Billie and Fitch and Owen." Luke pushed up his glasses. "Because they're Negroes." He said it quietly, like he was embarrassed to mention it.

Sam looked down. "Every place isn't like Mayfield."

I remembered Papa saying something like that. "Mayfield is special," was what he'd said.

"What was it like in the Navy?" I asked. "Were people nice?"

"Some people," Sam said. "And things were pretty good for me, especially at first. I made some friends, colored and white, just like here in Mayfield. But like Luke said, it wasn't so good for the Negroes sometimes. I had a hard time with that and said so. That's when I started having trouble myself."

" 'Cause you were sticking up for them?" Dillon asked.

Sam nodded.

"That's just like at Parkview," Alice said. "A girl there told me that I'd be better off if I stopped hanging around with . . ." She glanced up at me then looked down. "With Meg and them."

"When? Who?" Mo asked, like she couldn't believe it.

"It doesn't matter," Alice said. "I just told her that the *world* would be better off if *she* wasn't in it."

Everybody laughed. That Alice. She always spoke her mind, even when it could get her in Dutch. People with red hair are supposed to be hot tempered. All the Clearys had red hair, but Alice was the quickest to get mad.

"It isn't everybody at Parkview," Mo said. "Some people are nice. Like Mr. Callahan, Mr. Stanley, and Ivy."

I nodded, glad she thought that, too. "Yeah, things are better now." I looked at Billie, remembering what he'd said the night the World Series ended. "Just watch out."

In September when school first started, the Parkview kids treated us Mayfielders like we had the plague or something. Ivy Scott was the first one to be friendly to us. Clayton Reed and some other Parkview kids didn't like it, but Ivy stood up to them. After that, a lot of the other kids treated us better, too. We played ball together and ate at the same lunch table sometimes.

And during the World Series, I was believing that our troubles were over. The whole school was rooting for the Pittsburgh Pirates, and all anybody ever talked about was who their favorite player was and what had happened in the latest game. The Parkview kids, even Clayton, forgot about calling us names and making us feel like we didn't belong. Except one time when Billie was talking about how great Roberto Clemente is, and Clayton said, "Clemente's all right, for a colored guy."

Billie looked mad for a minute, then let it go. That kind of talk had ended in a fight with Clayton before, and Billie and I had gotten into trouble with Principal Callahan and with Mama and Papa, too. Billie had a temper, and Papa had given him strict orders to control it.

The Series was tied, three games apiece, and on the day of the seventh game Mr. Callahan set up a TV in the big main hallway and allowed the whole school to watch. We had to stay with our own classes, so the Mayfield crew couldn't all sit together, but we stuck as close as we could. Billie was with Luke and Dillon in the sixth grade. Alice kept with the twins in the fifth grade. And I was next to Mo in fourth. Ivy and another Parkview girl, Jane Monroe, were with Mo and me, too.

During commercials, the teachers would let us yell, "Beat 'em Bucs!" but otherwise we had to keep pretty quiet. It got even quieter in the bottom of the ninth when the Pirates and the Yankees were tied at nine runs each. Kids were biting their fingernails and holding on to each other when Bill Mazeroski really clobbered one. "Kiss it good-bye!" I said to myself like the radio announcer Bob Prince.

It was the home run that won the game, and at Parkview it was like the end of a war or something. Everybody in the school—kids, teachers, the nurse, the secretary, and even Mr. Callahan—was jumping and screaming and hugging and laughing. Afterward we sang "Take Me Out to the Ball Game" like we were all real close, like there was never anything bad between us.

That night I'd said to Billie, "I think it's going to be okay at Parkview. Don't you?"

Billie was quiet for a while. Then I heard him shift in his bed. "It's better, Meg," he said. "But . . ."

It got quiet again.

"But, what?"

"Just watch out, that's all."

"For what?" I started to say, but I knew the conversation was over. I faced the wall, disappointed. I'd wanted him to agree with me because my brother was right about most things. I said a little prayer that he'd be wrong this time.

Now, listening to the rest of the gang talk about Parkview, listening to Sam, I knew Billie had been right. Maybe the Lord was busy that night taking care of other important business. I closed my eyes and prayed that Mr. Stanley would hurry up and get better.

Chapter 5

The snow seemed to melt as fast as it had come, and two days later we were back in school. Mrs. Davis sat at the teacher's desk like she wasn't leaving any time soon.

If someone'd asked me why I felt nervous around Mrs. Davis, I don't know that I'd have an answer. She was real smart and she never yelled, but, for some reason, I wasn't sure if she liked me.

This morning Mrs. Davis was talking about the Civil War and President Abraham Lincoln.

"Mr. Lincoln issued the Emancipation Proclamation and set free the slaves in the South," Mrs. Davis said. "The Thirteenth Amendment, which was passed later, outlawed all slavery throughout the nation."

Some kids turned around and looked at me. Every time the word "slavery" or "Negro" came up, I became the center of attention. I had gotten used it.

I looked down at my opened history book and drew a little circle on the page.

"Margaret Turner," Mrs. Davis said.

"Yes, ma'am." I focused my eyes on her forehead. She walked over to my desk and looked at my book.

"We do not put marks in our books," she said. "Would someone like to tell Margaret why."

Nobody needed to tell me, but I didn't say anything.

Clayton Reed, who sat right behind me, raised his hand.

"Clayton?"

"Because they—"

"We do not begin a sentence with 'because'," Mrs. Davis said, turning to face him.

Clayton coughed and started again. "We do not put marks in our books because they don't belong to us. They belong to the school and the school belongs to the taxpayers. And the taxpayers—"

"That will be enough, Clayton. Thank you." Mrs. Davis looked back at me. "I realize that you haven't been at Parkview very long, and so I will overlook this. I'm sure there are rules here to which you might not be accustomed."

I'd been there since September, so I knew the rules. "I know I shouldn't have written in the book," I said. I wanted her to know that I didn't write in books at Mayfield School or at home either. "I wasn't thinking," I said.

"Well, we think in this classroom." She was smiling. "Don't we, children?"

"Yes, Mrs. Davis," some kids answered in a singsong way.

My face felt hot.

"Now erase these marks, Margaret."

"Yes, ma'am."

I glanced at Mo, seated two rows over, and could see the sorry in her eyes.

It was almost time for music class and I was glad. I felt like I couldn't breathe, like something was sucking all the air out of the room.

The bell rang, but everyone stayed in their seats. "Teachers, not bells, are in charge," they all said, even Mr. Stanley.

"Before you leave . . ." Mrs. Davis said.

I could hear Clayton sigh behind me. He wanted to get to music. It was one of the few times I ever agreed with him.

"I had a silver pen on my desk that appears to be missing," Mrs. Davis went on. "It is extremely valuable and I ask that anyone who finds it or knows of its whereabouts speak with me directly." She looked serious, then her face got softer. "Don't be afraid of consequences. I only want the pen returned."

Some kids started looking around like they were trying to figure out who might have it.

26

Mrs. Davis smiled. "And just one more thing, then I'll let you go."

Clayton was about to jump plumb out of his seat.

"I know you are all wondering how you did on the surprise spelling quiz last week," Mrs. Davis said. "I'll be returning them after lunch, but I will tell you now that Maureen Cleary and Margaret Turner received the highest marks. Congratulations, girls!"

Mo smiled at me. We knew we'd done well. We had studied the words together for three nights in a row because we didn't know when the quiz would be.

I felt good and not good at the same time. I couldn't explain it. I wanted to be mad at Mrs. Davis for what she'd said about thinking, for making it seem like I didn't know it was wrong to write in my history book. I wanted to be mad, but I couldn't be. She'd been so nice about the spelling quiz.

Chapter 6

I kept praying for Mr. Stanley to get better and come back. He didn't, but Mrs. Davis never mentioned writing in the book again, and, for a while, things seemed okay with her.

Then one morning in May, I got to school and found her looking inside my desk. She stopped when she saw me.

"You keep a very neat desk, Margaret," she said. "You'll make a good housekeeper someday."

Something didn't feel right, but all I could say was, "Thank you, ma'am."

I didn't think anything more about it until I found the pen. It was the same day that our penmanship teacher, Mr. Painter, came.

"Very nice, Margaret, but you need to slant your ovals a bit more," Mr. Painter said. He came to the school once a month and visited each class. In between, we were supposed to practice our cursive writing.

Part of practicing was making ovals. When we did ovals, Mr. Painter would say, "Ready? Pencils touching paper. Now, begin, and round and around and around and around—keep those arms moving—round and around and around. Now lift and begin again, round and around and around and, Jane, loosen up on that pencil and around and around . . ."

When we were done, we were supposed to have a row of neat ovals across the page. Our whole arm was supposed to move while our wrists stayed stiff and we couldn't lift our pencils unless we were starting a new oval. Mr. Painter said doing ovals would help us make better letters.

Mr. Painter came around looking at everyone's paper, telling each of us what we were doing wrong so we'd know what to work on. We would turn in our papers today to be graded. I'd been getting mostly B pluses in handwriting. I needed to practice slanting, and I had a hard time keeping all my ovals the same size, but everything else seemed okay. Mr. Painter stepped over to Ivy's desk and showed her how to keep her wrist still and "let your arm do the work."

Then he looked up and announced, "As I check individual papers, you may begin writing our sentence." It was always the same: **The quick brown fox jumped over the lazy yellow dogs.** I used to think we wrote that because Mr. Painter liked animals, but I found out it was because the sentence had every letter in the alphabet.

"Very nice!" Mr. Painter told Clayton. "But then you've had plenty of practice." I knew he meant that Clayton was eleven and still in the fourth grade. I didn't think Mr. Painter meant to be mean, but if I was Clayton, I'd have felt bad.

I was real curious to see Clayton's paper, though. I dropped my pencil so I could bend down and maybe get a peek.

"What are you looking at?" Clayton asked in his smart-aleck way. His straight black hair hung over his eyes.

"I . . . your ovals. They're good," I said, and quickly faced forward again.

"Yeah, well this is baby stuff." He pulled my hair.

I flipped my pigtails to the front and leaned forward to practice the sentence.

I glanced across the room at Mo's freckled face. She saw me and smiled. It was like the sun coming from behind the clouds on a gray day. I smiled back and looked out the window. Spring had come, it was staying daylight longer, and we were playing baseball again. Things felt right.

I looked back at my paper, remembering not to hold my pencil too tight, and started the sentence—**The quick bro . . .**

A loud siren shrieked. It was an air-raid drill. I knew what to do—duck and cover.

I dropped my pencil, ducked under my desk, and covered my head with my arms. Everyone else did the same thing. We stayed like that for a while, then Mrs. Davis blew a whistle twice and everybody got back into their seats. This was usually the end of the drill, but today Mrs. Davis blew the whistle twice more. My heart pounded and I tugged my pigtail, wondering if this was a real air raid.

Some people said that Pittsburgh was sure to be the first target of the Russians because of all the steel factories, and steel was used to make stuff for the Army. Pittsburgh was close by. But I thought maybe the Russians would rather bomb Washington, D.C., first and get rid of the President and all the other people who told the country what to do when things went wrong.

Mrs. Davis looked like a traffic cop as she directed each row to "walk briskly but don't run" out of the room. Staying close to the walls, we walked single file through the halls and down the steps to the basement. I shivered. The basement smelled musty and there wasn't much light. There were fat twisty pipes, and a huge boiler furnace squatted in a corner down there. The furnace made strange hissing sounds and, in the shadows, looked like it had a monster face.

Everyone sat on the floor and waited for Mr. Callahan to blow his whistle telling us to go back to class. We weren't allowed to talk at all during the drill, but I always wanted to. It would have made me less nervous about being there.

So I always sang a song in my head. It was the duck-and-cover song from the air-raid movie the teachers showed to all the classes at the beginning of the year:

> *There was a turtle by the name of Bert*
> *And Bert the Turtle was very alert*
> *When danger threatened him he never got hurt*
> *He knew just what to do*
> *He'd duck and cover*
> *Duck and cover*
> *He did what we all must learn to do*
> *You and you and you and you*
> *You and you and you and you*
> *You and you and you and you*
> *Duck and cover*

I liked the "you and you and you and you" part. When I was singing it in my head, I'd pick out kids to point to, but I didn't really point. By the time I finished the song, Mr. Callahan gave the signal.

When we got back to our classroom, I ran over to Mo and hugged her, glad that there was no atomic bomb today, wondering what would happen if there really was one.

Chapter 7

As I was going to my seat, I remembered. When the air-raid siren blew and I got under my desk, I'd seen something shiny on the floor under the dictionary shelves. My desk was in the row right next to the dictionaries. I hadn't really thought about what the shiny thing might be at the time. All I could think about was the air raid. But now, I wondered if it might have been the silver pen, the one that Mrs. Davis was looking for.

Mrs. Davis was at the door talking to Billie's teacher, Mrs. Carmichael, when the lunch bell rang. She nodded to the class and everyone headed for the cloakroom to get their lunches. I got on my knees and peeked under the shelves. The pen wasn't too far under, so I could see it right away. I reached in and picked it up. It was real pretty and looked valuable like Mrs. Davis said. It was all silver except the little part that clips to your shirt pocket was gold.

With a pen like that, maybe I could write as good as Clayton. I started to put it in my pocket. Not to keep, just so I could try it out, just so I could show it to Mo. But I got this feeling in my stomach that, even if I planned on giving it back, it wouldn't be right. Besides, maybe Mrs. Davis would be so glad to get it back, she'd start to like me more. I walked right up to her just as Mrs. Carmichael was leaving.

"Excuse me, Mrs. Davis, but I found your pen, I think," I said, handing it to her.

Mrs. Davis took the pen, looked at it closely and said, "Thank you for returning it, Margaret. It was the right thing to do."

"You're welcome, ma'am," I said, smiling.

"Now go and get your lunch," she said.

After we got in line, Mrs. Davis said, "I have good news. The missing silver pen has been returned."

Clayton raised his hand and asked, "Who found it?"

"That isn't important right now," she said.

I didn't know what I'd expected, but the good feeling I had about finding the pen left me. I guess I wanted everyone to know it was me. I guess I wanted to be a hero. Then I remembered that Mama always said it meant more when you did a good deed that nobody knew about but God. I figured Mrs. Davis must know this, too, and didn't want to spoil the value of it. So I marched out of the room feeling good.

That is until Mo asked at lunch, "What would you do if there was a real bomb?" and started me thinking all over again.

Chapter 8

When Mo asked about the bomb, the spooky school basement came back into my mind.

"I wouldn't want to stay here." I picked up the other half of my peanut butter sandwich. "I'd want to go home."

All the Mayfield kids were there, plus Ivy, Jane, Clayton, and Judd Watson, who was in Billie's class.

"Well, that's dumb," Clayton said. He and Judd sat near us sometimes. I'm not sure why. All Clayton seemed to do was disagree with us, though he didn't call us names like he used to. Mr. Callahan had seen to that. Judd didn't say much. He just hung around Clayton all the time.

Billie bit his lip, but didn't say anything. Papa had warned us that Clayton would do stuff just to get us mad and that the way to win was *not* to get mad. I saw Papa's point, but it was hard. Sometimes you couldn't help wanting to argue with Clayton, or worse.

"What's so dumb about it?" Ivy asked, keeping her eyes on her baloney sandwich. She said it in her calm, quiet way. If it had been Alice, she'd have yelled.

Jane shook her curly hair and said, "Yeah?"

I smiled to myself. Jane went along with what Ivy said. Sort of like me and Mo.

"If you don't know, you must be as dumb as her," Clayton said. He leaned forward over the table. "By the time she got home, she'd have radiation all over her. And she'd be dead in a week. You have to wait at least fourteen days before you can go outside."

I didn't know if this was true, but I had heard that you couldn't see or smell or taste or feel radiation, and if it got on you, there was no way to get rid of it.

Clayton locked his hands behind his head and leaned back in his chair. "I can understand why you'd want to go home, though. That's what I'd do."

"But you said—" Alice started to argue.

"It's different for me," he said, cutting her off. "I've got protection—a radiation suit. Here at school."

Nobody said anything. We just sat there, confused.

Clayton rocked on the back legs of his chair and smiled.

"So where is it?" Luke asked, breaking the silence. "Show us."

"I'm not telling. If I told you and the Russians bombed us, you'd all try to get it."

Luke laughed and said, "He's bluffing."

Clayton stood up. "You calling me a liar?"

My stomach felt tight. Why was Clayton always looking for a fight?

"I'm just saying, prove it," Luke said. He didn't sound mad, just matter-of-fact.

"Yeah, prove it," said Ivy.

"Yeah," Jane said.

Clayton laughed. "Okay, you all want proof. Ask Mr. Callahan. That proof enough for you?"

Mr. Callahan? What did he have to do with it?

Everybody seemed to have the same question because all eyes were focused on Clayton.

You could tell he loved being the center of attention. He sat back down and kept us waiting for a minute.

"Let's go hit some balls before recess is over," Billie said, breaking the spell.

Everyone agreed and started to gather up their lunch bags, wax paper, and apple cores from the table.

When Clayton realized he'd lost the spotlight, he quickly blurted out, "My dad asked Mr. Callahan to keep the suit in a safe place for me. Mr. Callahan's supposed to send me home on my bike after the explosion."

As much as I didn't want to be, I was impressed. It sounded like it might be true.

We all stood listening while he finished. "The suit's real

heavy because it's lined with lead cloth, and there's a gas mask attached so I can breathe good air. It's locked up in the basement with my bike."

It got quiet again, then Dillon said, "I don't know why everybody's worried about the Russians bombing us anyway. My brother, Sam, says it'll never happen. He says that if *they* bomb us, we have the time to bomb *them* even before their bombs hit. The Russians know it'd be suicide. That's what Sam says. He says the atomic bomb is really a weapon of peace, not war."

Mr. Stanley had talked about the Soviet Union when we'd had our first air-raid drill earlier in the year. He'd said something like that, too, and I thought it made sense, but Clayton said, "You think your brother knows everything. Well, that's a buncha crap. The Russians are crazy. If they get mad enough, they'll do anything. They don't care about getting bombed as long as they get us. All it takes is one person"—he held up his pointing finger—"one crazy Russian, to push the button. Even if other Russians don't want him to, it'll be too late." He looked at Dillon. "What does your know-it-all brother say about that?"

Everybody looked at Dillon. I sat back down. Some of the others did, too. We weren't going to the ball field just yet.

"He says the Russians are people just like us," Dillon said.

"Oh yeah?" Clayton said. "If they're just like us, how

come they have to use spies to steal our secrets? How come they couldn't make their own atomic bomb? How come they had to copy from us? I'll tell you why. Because they're not as smart as us. And my dad says that's what makes them dangerous."

"How?" Fitch asked. He and Owen hadn't said a word since this started. They had become pretty quiet at school since we'd come to Parkview.

"The dumber you are the more you're likely to do something crazy," Clayton said. "And my dad says it's dangerous to think the Russians are just like us because we'll let our guard down. That's how they'll get us."

I couldn't help asking, "But why do they want to get us?"

"Because they hate us. They want everybody to be Communists like them. Communists don't like us being free to say what we want 'cause it makes them look bad." Clayton seemed to have all the answers.

"In Russia," he said, "if you say something against the government, something like, 'I wish they'd give us more food to eat,' soldiers arrest you. You could spend the rest of your life in prison or they might put you in a gas chamber or even just shoot you right there."

Blah, blah, blah. I was tired of listening. Even if it was true, I didn't want to hear. I thought about covering my ears, but Clayton seemed to have run out of steam, and Dillon was smart enough to let him have the last word.

There wasn't much time left, but we all grabbed our gloves and headed out to the ball field anyway to practice hitting and catching. All except Clayton and Judd. Clayton had been talking so much he hadn't eaten his lunch. I think Judd wanted to play, but he stayed behind with Clayton.

I took my usual position as catcher with Billie pitching. I liked having a fence behind me so I didn't have to go chasing balls that I missed. In Mayfield, we never had a real field. The one at Parkview was the best we'd ever played on. Everybody walked onto the field and took their places, Luke at first, Dillon at second, and Owen at third, with Fitch in between at shortstop. The twins always stuck together. Alice and Ivy took the outfield. Jane sat on the bleachers and watched. Mo usually played outfield, but today she was at home plate hitting balls to us.

Owen had been quiet all during lunch, but now he said, "Nothing like a game to keep us from going insane."

"Yeah," Billie said, pitching me a ball.

I knew what they meant. After all that talk about Russians, it felt good to be back on the field. The ball stung my hand right through my mitt, and I wondered would a radiation suit be like wearing a baseball glove all over, or would it be more like a space suit?

Chapter 9

As we were going back to class after lunch recess, Mrs. Davis touched my shoulder and motioned me to step out of line.

"Mr. Callahan would like to speak with you, Margaret," she said quietly.

I tugged my pigtail. I liked Mr. Callahan. He was real nice and he was fair. Sometimes he'd ask me questions about Mayfield Crossing, not just out of politeness, but really wanting to know. Still, he was the principal, and I had a feeling that he wouldn't be calling me away from class unless there was something wrong.

I walked to his office and sat down in the waiting chair next to his secretary, Miss Myers. Everybody knew to sit in the waiting chair until Miss Myers said Mr. Callahan was ready. I looked at her face hoping to get a clue about why I was there. I don't know why I bothered. Miss Myers was an expert at not letting her feelings show. She got up and peeked into his office. Then she looked at me, nodded, and held the door open while I walked in. I sat in a chair facing Mr. Callahan's huge desk.

"Good afternoon, Meg," he said with a smile. His thick eyebrows were so close together they looked like one.

"Good afternoon, sir," I said, hoping that maybe he only wanted to ask me some more questions about Mayfield after all.

But just as I started to relax, Mrs. Davis came in and closed the door behind her.

"I'm sorry I'm late. I wanted to give the students some work so that Tom, ah, Mr. Nolan would only have to monitor." She sat down in the chair next to mine.

I must have looked confused or worried because Mr. Callahan asked, "Meg, don't you know why you're here today?"

"No, sir," I said.

Mrs. Davis reached over and patted the back of my hand. "Now, Margaret, let's be truthful about this."

I didn't know what to say because I didn't know what she meant.

Mr. Callahan cleared his throat. "Mrs. Davis told me that you returned a pen that had disappeared from her desk."

"Yes, sir," I said.

"She seems to think that the pen was not simply misplaced but deliberately taken. We hoped you could tell us how you came to have it."

I swallowed hard to keep from throwing up. They thought I stole it. I couldn't talk for a minute. I focused my eyes on the stapler on Mr. Callahan's desk. Finally I managed to say, "Under the dictionary shelves."

"Excuse me?" Mrs. Davis said.

I looked up at Mr. Callahan. "I found it under the dictionary shelves next to my desk. It was right before lunch . . . right before I gave it to Mrs. Davis."

Mr. Callahan opened his mouth like he was going to say something, but before he could, Mrs. Davis asked, "And how did you know the pen was under the bookshelves? What were you doing crawling around on the floor?"

"It was when the air raid started," I said.

"Now, Margaret, first you said you found it right before lunch. Now you say it was during the air-raid drill. Which is it?"

I took a deep breath. For a second I thought I'd start crying, but something kept me from it. I was too mad to cry. I looked Mrs. Davis right in the eyes and said, "I saw it when I was under my desk for duck and cover. But I didn't even know that what I saw was the pen. It was shiny, that's all. And I didn't get it until after the drill because I didn't have time to think about it. Mr. Stanley always said we're not supposed to think about other stuff during an air-raid drill."

"Mr. Stanley is correct, Meg," Mr. Callahan said, nodding. "And you were right to wait until after the crisis, or potential crisis, was over."

I looked at him now and continued. "When I got back, I remembered I'd seen something, so I looked under the shelves. That's when I found the pen and gave it to Mrs. Davis."

"Now, Margaret," Mrs. Davis began. If she said "now, Margaret" one more time I'd scream. "Remember I said not to worry about consequences. I'm just pleased to have the pen back. Mr Callahan and I are not planning to punish you. We simply feel—"

Mr. Callahan coughed and Mrs. Davis shifted in her seat. "*I* simply feel that it's important for the individual to take reponsibility for his or her actions," she said, "to be truthful and gain from the experience. Perhaps you haven't learned that where you come from."

I looked at Mrs. Davis's face. She was sure I was guilty. I remembered the day I found her looking in my desk. She thought I'd stolen the pen even before I'd found it.

I turned to Mr. Callahan, but I could hardly see him because my eyes were filling up. "I didn't do anything wrong!" I said, almost shouting. I tried to stay mad so I wouldn't cry.

"And there's no proof that you did," he said. "Is there, Mrs. Davis?"

"Perhaps not," she said. "But we know the truth, don't we, Margaret?"

I didn't answer. I was afraid I'd say something I shouldn't, something I'd be sorry for later.

Finally, Mr. Callahan said, "Mrs. Davis, don't you think you should be returning to your students? I'd like a few moments with Meg. I'll send her back to class when we're finished."

"Well," she said to me, "perhaps you'll feel more comfortable talking with Mr. Callahan about it." She started to pat my hand again, but I moved it away. I didn't want her to touch me.

Mr. Callahan walked her to the door and closed it. Then he came and sat down in the chair she'd been in. He let out a breath, like he was real tired. It got quiet.

"I didn't take the pen, Mr. Callahan. Honest, I found it just like I said."

"I know, Meg."

I studied his face. He believed me.

"Then why am I here?" I asked.

"I needed to hear your side, that's all," he said.

He handed me a Kleenex. "Thanks, Mr. Callahan," I said, blowing my nose. "But Mrs. Davis . . . she thinks . . ."

"I know," he said, "and I'm sorry to have to say that it is your word against her suspicions. You're just going to have to let this go, Meg."

"Why doesn't she like me, Mr. Callahan?" Finally, I said it out loud.

He looked out the window. "It isn't you, Meg." Then he turned back to me and said, "I'm going to tell you a secret."

Mr. Callahan? Tell *me* a secret? "In Mayfield we *always* keep secrets," was all I could think of to say.

"I know, that's why I believe I can trust you."

He leaned closer and whispered, "Mr. Stanley is coming back *very* soon."

I almost screamed out loud. "Mr. Stanley? When?"

"Just soon," he said, "so you needn't worry about what Mrs. Davis thinks. You can return to class now."

On the way, I tried to do what Mr. Callahan said. I tried to let go of the bad feeling I had about Mrs. Davis. It was still there, but I smiled, thinking about Mr. Stanley and wishing "very soon" meant this minute.

Chapter 10

On the bus, I sat next to Mo as always, but Billie squeezed in next to me.

"What were you doing in Mr. Callahan's office?" he asked right away.

Sometimes I thought my brother had hired someone in the fourth grade to spy on me. Before I could say anything, Mo answered Billie's question.

"It was for something good," she said. My mouth fell open. "Meg found Mrs. Davis's missing silver pen that was real valuable. Mr. Callahan was just telling Meg how proud he was of her."

"Who told you that?" I couldn't help asking.

"Some kids in class," Mo said.

Billie smiled at me. "Really?"

"It was no big deal," I whispered. I didn't want to talk about it. Not on the bus where somebody else might hear.

Billie studied my face, then said, "That was real nice, Meg," and went to sit in his usual seat with Luke.

Mo squeezed my hand and looked out the window. She had gotten the message, too.

Finally she turned to me and said, "Did you believe all that stuff Clayton was goin' on about?"

"Oh, he's just a big windbag," Alice said from the seat behind. "He said Sam was a know-it-all. *He's* the one who was being a know-it-all. Maybe he does have some dumb old suit, but I don't care."

I couldn't say it out loud, but inside I *did* care, a little anyway.

"Let's not talk about Clayton," I said.

"Okay with me," Alice said. "Hey, wanna play Hula Hoops later?"

"Maybe," I said.

We didn't say much the rest of the way home, but when we got off the bus at the Mayfield stop, the whole gang gathered around me and wanted to know what really happened. I told them everything, except about Mr. Stanley coming back.

"Who does she think she is, accusing you like that?" Alice yelled.

"She's just like Miss Derry," Fitch said, shaking his head. "Always thinkin' Owen and me are cheatin'."

"It's good that the other kids don't know the real reason

you were in Mr. Callahan's office," Luke said. "It would be all over the school."

Mo sighed. "I wish Mr. Stanley would come back."

"Me, too," I said, wishing I didn't have to keep such a good secret from my best friend.

Billie squeezed my shoulder. "You gonna tell Mama and Papa?"

"I just want to forget it," I said.

We all did a spit handshake and swore we wouldn't tell anybody about the pen and Mrs. Davis. As we split up to go home, everybody gave me a pat on the arm or a pigtail tug and I felt better. But by the time Billie and I got to our porch, I was wondering if Mr. Callahan had called Mama on the telephone.

Chapter 11

The principal usually called home when there was some problem at school. I didn't think he would this time, since I wasn't in any trouble. But I knew I should tell Mama about the pen anyway.

Billie yelled, "We're home," and headed for the bedroom to change clothes and do homework like always.

When I walked into the kitchen and saw Mama standing at the stove stirring spaghetti sauce, all I wanted was for her to hold me real tight. I hugged her from behind. I wanted to tell her about the pen, but when I opened my mouth, something else that was on my mind came out.

"Mama, can Billie and I get radiation suits and bicycles to have at school so that if there's an atomic bomb we can come home?"

She put the lid on the sauce pan and turned around, laughing.

"Meg, what on earth are you talking about?"

I knew I shouldn't believe anything Clayton said, but somehow, I couldn't get it out of my mind. If he *was* right, I wanted one of those suits. It bothered me that Mama was laughing. I looked down because my eyes were filling up.

Mama stooped down in front of me. "I'm sorry, honey. I didn't realize you were serious."

She led me to a kitchen chair, sat down, and pulled me onto her lap. I was getting big for this, but it felt good to be in Mama's arms. She smelled sweet, like lilacs. It was the cologne Billie and I had given her for Mother's Day the day before. We'd put our money together and bought it at the G. C. Murphy five-and-ten.

I put my arms around Mama's neck and told her all about what Clayton had said, what Dillon had said, and about the scary basement.

By the time I finished, I was crying. "So I want one of those radiation suits so that I can come home and be with you and Papa. Billie, too." I felt like a big baby, but I didn't care. Nobody saw me but Mama.

She brushed back my bangs, held me tight, and rocked me a little.

"First of all, about the radiation suit," Mama said. "People who work with uranium have to wear special suits for protection, so there probably is such a thing. And Clayton may or may not have one.

"Second," she went on, "I think Sam is right. The Russians are smart enough to realize the consequences of a nuclear war, that the whole world, including their own country, would be in danger."

"But what if—"

She put her finger to my lips. "Most important, if there *were* an attack of some kind, your father and I would come get you." She looked me in the eyes and, real serious, said, "I promise. So all you'll have to do is wait with Billie and Mr. Stanley and Mr. Callahan and Mo and all your friends at the school until we get there. And we *will* get there. Do you believe me?"

I studied Mama's face. She looked sure and determined, like the Lone Ranger when he was going after the bad guys, or Superman when he was fighting for truth, justice, and the American way.

I wiped my face with my hand and nodded. I almost told her about the pen, but she scooted me off her lap and said, "You go on now and change your school clothes." When she went back to the stove, I saw her wipe the side of her eye with her apron.

I put on play clothes, then started my homework with Billie.

"Done yet?" I asked when I was finished with mine.

"No." He sounded tired. "Go on without me."

I didn't want to, so I flopped down on my bed.

Billie always had lots of homework. He'd gotten straight A's at the old Mayfield School, but it was harder for him at Parkview. His teacher, Mrs. Carmichael, always seemed to find some little something wrong with his papers. Billie said she was real nice to him when she found a mistake, but was kind of mean when she didn't. That didn't make any sense to me at all. Wasn't the teacher supposed to want you to do well?

I said he should tell Mama and Papa, but he didn't. Not until he got his report card and had a B in History. He told Mama and Papa it was because of his oral report. He was real nervous giving it and it counted for a lot of his grade that time. Mrs. Carmichael took off points for "presentation," he'd said. Then he'd gotten mad and crumpled up his written report. He'd smoothed it out and copied it over, but Mrs. Carmichael told him she didn't like his attitude.

Mama and Papa talked to Mrs. Carmichael about it, and things got a little better, but Papa told Billie, "Mrs. Carmichael is your teacher, and I want you to be respectful and to do the very best you can."

Then he said, "Both you and Meg must realize that as Negroes you will face people like this all of your lives, people *you* will have to educate."

"Don't you have to go to college to be a teacher?" I asked.

"Not that kind of educating, Meg," Billie said. I always wondered how my brother knew so much.

"What your father is saying is that some people won't believe you're as smart or as good as everybody else because you're colored," Mama said. "So you'll have to work harder to show them."

I watched Billie write something on his homework paper. It wasn't fair that he had to work harder. I got up from my bed and looked out of the window, wondering why people didn't want to believe we're smart. Then I remembered what Clayton said at lunch about the Russians. About them not being as smart as Americans and about them being dangerous because of it. Did he think *we* were dangerous, too? Was that why Mrs. Davis thought I'd steal her pen?

Just then something moving outside caught my eye. It was Old Hairy. I hadn't really been looking at anything, just staring in the direction of the woods, so he'd caught me off guard.

I sucked in air and ducked below the window ledge. Even though I wasn't as afraid of him as I used to be, all those years of dodging had made it a reflex. The minute I saw overalls, flannel shirt, and whiskers, my body just wanted to hide somewhere.

"Billie," I whispered. He looked over. "Mr. Slater." I pointed up at the window from below. Mama had told us we weren't allowed to call him Old Hairy anymore. She said it was disrespectful. Billie hit the floor, too, and crawled over. Then we both slowly eased up until we could peek out.

Old Hairy was walking down the road toward the woods where his cabin was supposed to be. At least that's where Sam and Frank said it was. Old Hairy usually just had his knapsack on his back. But today he had a pick and shovel balanced on one shoulder.

He looked over at us and I almost ducked again, but he held up his hand in a wave. I waved back. Billie did, too. Even though we liked to keep our distance, Old Hairy was still a part of Mayfield. He turned and kept walking.

Billie went back to his homework and I lay down on my bed. Old Hairy hadn't been around lately, and I wondered what he was up to. There were all kinds of things he might be doing with a pick and shovel, but I forced myself not to think about them. Instead, I went over to the Clearys' to play Hula Hoops.

Chapter 12

Mo and Alice hadn't finished their homework yet either, so I decided to work on the village until they could come out.

The village was sort of a forever project in our backyard. We used little houses from Billie's train set and miniature cars and toy farm animals and made a little town. We'd scrape roads into the dirt and use whatever we could find, like sticks and pebbles, to stand for different things. Sometimes we'd make a park with flowers. I'd even made a swimming pool once with a jar lid I wedged into the ground. After winter was over or when it rained, we'd usually have to start all over, but we didn't mind. We'd just pretend there had been a flood or an earthquake.

I noticed some ants had built a hill right in the middle of one of the roads I'd made last time. The ants were running in and out carrying little bits of things, I couldn't tell what. Sometimes we'd put some sugar on the ground and watch while hundreds of ants came and took it away a grain at a time.

"Don't worry," I said to them. "You can stay there." And I started to scrape a detour around the anthill.

"Now this is nice!"

I jerked in surprise and looked up. Sam was smiling down at me. "Didn't mean to scare you."

"It's okay," I said, my heart slowing down. Sometimes Old Hairy would turn up real sudden like that.

Sam stooped down and started asking about the village, so I explained what everything was. It had been nearly three months since Lucky'd come back, so we'd all gotten pretty used to calling him Sam.

"Where'd you get these?" he asked, picking up two cars made of walnut shells with pencil erasers for wheels.

"Mr. Slater left them for us one day."

"Hmm," Sam said. He placed the cars back on the road. "Are you kids still telling Old Hairy stories?"

"Not much anymore," I said. "Mama doesn't like it. Besides, he isn't so bad."

Sam nodded. "Glad you figured that out so young. I never did, you know. Not until Frank . . ." His eyes looked sad, but then he changed the subject. "It's nice that you're letting the ants have some space in your village."

"What about Frank?" I couldn't let it go.

Sam stood up. "That was a long time ago. Just know,

Meg, that people aren't always what they seem. Harry Slater is an exceptional person." He turned and walked away. "See you later."

"Bye."

Mama once said that Old Hairy was "an original." Now Sam called him "exceptional." Were Fitch and Owen wrong about Old Hairy having something to do with Frank's death? Frank *did* die. So what had Old Hairy done that night that was so exceptional? I lined up the walnut cars on the road with all the others behind them. Then I went back to the Clearys' to get Mo and Alice.

"Sam said Old Hairy is exceptional," I told them as Mo and I watched Alice wiggle back and forth to keep the Hula Hoop going.

"That's 'cause he's a grown-up now," Alice said. "You know how they are. Anyway, how can Sam say that after what Old Hairy did to his best friend?"

"We don't know what happened to Frank," Mo argued.

"Fitch and Owen said when they went to the hospital to see Frank, he had bruises all over his face. Who else would have done *that*?" Alice asked. "And when they asked about the marks, Mrs. Sherman gave them one of those answers that don't mean nothing."

I knew what she meant. "Frank met with some trouble." But, I'd never heard anything about bruises. Alice was in the same grade as the twins. The older kids always seemed to know more than us about what was going on.

"But why would Old Hairy bring Frank home if he beat him up?" Mo asked.

"He's crazy," Alice said, calm as a still pond. "Crazy people do stuff like that."

"Do you think he ever gets lonely bein' by himself all the time?" I asked.

"Who? Old Hairy?" Alice rolled her eyes. "Meg Turner, you are getting more like your mama every day."

But Mo answered my question. "I guess everybody gets lonely sometimes, even Clayton."

Alice stopped and put her hand on her hips. "Now you're both making me sick." The Hula Hoop dropped to the ground.

"You were going good, Alice," I said. "Why did you stop?"

She pretended to look mad. "I coulda gone longer if I hadn't felt like throwing up on you two."

We started laughing.

"Hey!" Alice said, pointing. "There's Sam."

I turned around to see him coming our way.

"A Hula Hoop!" he said, smiling. "We had some good times with those."

"*You* played Hula Hoops?" Alice asked.

Sam nodded. "In the Navy. When they first came out, we had Hula Hoop contests."

"In the *Navy?*" Mo asked.

"Were you any good?" Alice asked.

"I was okay, I guess. Better than some, but . . ."

"Let's see." Alice handed Sam the hoop.

Sam slid it through his hands.

"Well, I don't know . . . It's been a couple of years . . ."

"Chicken?" Alice teased.

"Go ahead, Sam," Mo said.

Sam stepped into the hoop and held it at his waist. He looked at us, smiling, but a little embarrassed.

"Here goes," he said, whipping the hoop around his waist to get it started.

With Sam's long legs, his behind was higher than most, and he looked a little funny getting started. Alice giggled at first, but once Sam got a rhythm going, the hoop seemed to become part of him. It was quiet except for the sound of the hoop moving. The three of us stood watching, hypnotized by the motion.

Sam had been looking down, concentrating, but now he lifted his head and smiled so big my heart started pounding and I held my breath. If it had been the wind, that smile would've knocked me right over. I remembered seeing it when I was little, before Sam had left. But now I knew that, just like Samson's strength was in his long hair, Sam's power was in that smile. I believed he could do anything with it.

A laugh escaped my throat and we all came back from wherever Sam had taken us.

"Wow," Alice finally said. "He's the Hula Hoop king!"

Sam stopped the hoop with his hand and bowed. We all clapped.

"How do you—?" Mo started to ask.

"Teach us," Alice said at the same time.

"There's really nothing I can teach you girls. You already know how," he said. "But I *can* tell you one thing."

"What?" we asked.

"The secret to Hula Hoops," he said, "like most everything, is your state of mind."

He handed me the hoop. "Thanks. See you later."

We watched him walk over to my house and go in the back door.

"What did he mean?" Mo asked.

"Who knows?" Alice said.

Our eyes stayed stuck on the door for a moment, even though Sam was already inside.

"He's always over there talking to your dad, Meg," Alice said. "What do they talk about all the time?"

I shrugged. "Beats me."

Sometimes after bedtime, I'd hear a knock at the door and Papa would let Sam in. I'd go to sleep listening to the murmur of their low voices, but I couldn't hear what they were saying. And it wasn't just Papa he talked to. Sometimes he'd be there when Billie and I got home from school and Papa was still at work. Mama'd be doing her usual stuff in the kitchen, getting supper ready, and Sam'd be sitting at the table just talking away.

When Billie and I'd walk in, whatever they were saying would change to stuff like, "How was school today?" and then Sam would say it was about time he left Mama alone so she could tend to us and finish supper.

I put the Hula Hoop around my waist and gave it a swing with my hand to get it started.

"Your dad seems real interested in what Sam's gonna do now," Mo said, her eyes following the hoop around and around. "They're probably talking about that and other boring grown-up stuff, like work and politics."

"Probably," I said, but I *was* curious to know what was going on with Sam. He seemed like he had something on his mind all the time. Like there was something he needed to figure out. Something.

The Hula Hoop moved down below my waist and flopped to the ground. I'd lost my concentration. I'd have to work on my state of mind.

Chapter 13

After supper, Billie and I were doing the dishes and Mama and Papa were watching the news on television. We were hurrying to get finished because *My Pal Trigger* with Roy Rogers and Dale Evans was coming on the Million Dollar Movie. It was one of our favorites, and Mama said we could stay up to watch it if we finished our homework and the dishes were done.

As usual, Papa had held things up. He was a real slow eater. When everyone else was finished, he'd only be halfway done.

"You all eat so fast," he'd say. "I don't know how you have time to taste what's going down."

He was probably right, and I'd try to eat slow like him, but I'd always forget and before I knew it my plate'd be empty.

Anyway, Billie and I were hurrying so we weren't talking

much, and that's when I heard something about a bus being set on fire in Alabama. A bus with people in it.

I carried the plate I was drying over to the doorway between the kitchen and the living room so I could see the TV. A newsman was talking.

The mob of about one hundred white men armed with blackjacks, clubs, knives, and tire chains smashed the windows and slashed the tires of the Greyhound bus carrying the nine Negro and white Freedom Riders.

Billie stood behind me, listening, too.

Six miles outside of Anniston, Alabama, the tires went flat, forcing the bus into a gas station where the mob continued its attack, smashing a window and hurling a firebomb inside. Members of the mob surrounded the bus, some holding the door closed, until state police forced them to disperse. All passengers, including the Freedom Riders, escaped before the vehicle burst into flames. Twelve passengers were treated for smoke inhalation.

"What are they so mad about?" I asked.

"Shh," Billie said.

The Freedom Riders are members of CORE, the Congress on Racial Equality, the civil rights activist group, which organized the rides in an attempt to break down racial barriers in the Deep South.

Although federal courts have outlawed enforced seg-
regation among interstate passengers, many bus stations
in Alabama and other southern states still maintain sep-
arate white and Negro waiting areas.

According to a CORE spokeman, the Freedom Rides
will continue despite yesterday's attack on the bus.

In other news, the nation's florists yesterday reported
record sales to Mother's Day shoppers. Sales of roses . . .

Papa turned off the TV and went over and sat on the couch by Mama. He put his arm around her, and she leaned in real close. Billie and I went back to the sink to finish up. We didn't talk at first. Finally I asked, "Who are the Freedom Riders?"

"Didn't you hear, Meg? They're a civil rights group like the NAACP," Billie said.

"What's that stand for again?" I asked. I knew it was something about helping colored people.

"The National Association for the Advancement of Colored People. The Freedom Riders are doing the same sorta thing as the people at those sit-ins last year. Remember?"

I remembered. There'd been news reports about people, Negroes, being attacked and arrested for sitting at lunch counters in places like Woolworth's where colored people weren't supposed to eat. It wasn't fair. Why shouldn't they be able to buy a sandwich like anybody else? But I also wondered why they'd go to a place where they weren't wanted. Why they went to all that trouble.

"How come—?" I started to say, but Papa called us in. We weren't quite done putting the dishes away, but he didn't seem to care.

"Yes, Papa," Billie said.

I stood next to Billie, waiting for Papa to tell us about the Freedom Riders, to answer my questions like always. But he just said, "Your program's starting," then got up and turned the TV back on.

I looked at Mama. She had made the rules about the dishes. She took the tea towel from my hand and said, "We'll finish. You two go ahead and watch your movie."

She and Papa went into the kitchen, and Billie and I settled down to watch. Soon we were riding the range with Roy and Dale and Trigger, and by the time it was over, we just lay on the rug talking about our favorite parts and about who was better, Roy Rogers or Hopalong Cassidy.

I had forgotten all about Freedom Riders, mobs, and burning buses. But they would come back to me much sooner than I knew.

Chapter 14

The next day started out good.

"Mr. Stanley will be back tomorrow," Mrs. Davis announced just before lunch. Everybody cheered.

I grinned across the room at Mo and she grinned back.

"We've accomplished a great deal together," Mrs. Davis said, "and to celebrate and say good-bye, I made some treats for you to have with your lunch." We all cheered again.

The third-grade teacher appeared at the door holding a tray of chocolate cupcakes topped with pink frosting.

We had our lunch, ate cupcakes, and Mrs. Davis didn't make us do any hard schoolwork for the rest of the day. We had a spelling bee that was just for fun, then Mrs. Davis read to us while we drew pictures and did jigsaw puzzles.

At the end of the day, she called kids up to her desk to return the friendly letters she'd assigned for homework the week before. When she called my name I went up smiling. She was being so nice, I wasn't even thinking about the pen.

"This is a well-written letter, Margaret. Your punctuation and capitalization are correct."

"Thank you, Mrs. Davis," I said.

"Your penmanship is improving, but remember to slant your letters a bit more."

"Yes, ma'am."

"You are a good student, Margaret."

"Thank you, ma'am."

Mrs. Davis didn't speak for a moment. She had been looking at my paper the whole time, and now she looked right at me. She still didn't say anything, but she hadn't said I could go back to my seat yet.

Finally she asked, "Is there anything you'd like to say to me, Margaret, before I leave?" She opened her desk drawer, took out the silver pen, and held it in her hand.

I studied her face and saw the same thing I did that day in Mr. Callahan's office. She still wanted me to say I stole it.

My eyes filled up, but I didn't let myself cry.

"No," was all I said, and without being dismissed, I walked back to my seat. I didn't even say "ma'am" like Mama'd taught me.

I was glad Mrs. Davis was leaving and I wished I hadn't eaten her cupcake. I propped my English book up on my desk so she couldn't see my face and pretended to read. I didn't know what to do with the mad I was feeling, so I breathed in and out real slow. Then I thought about tomorrow. Mr. Stanley would be back and everything would be okay.

After school we were all standing in the rocky field we used for baseball and all our other games in Mayfield. I was looking forward to some good hitting.

"Where's Dillon?" Luke asked, punching his glove. "Isn't he coming?"

"He said he'd play, and maybe he'd bring Sam today," Owen said.

Alice swung the bat. "Maybe Sam doesn't want to and Dillon's trying to talk him into it. Maybe we should just warm up until he gets here."

"No," Billie said, looking at Dillon's house. "We'll wait just like always."

"Maybe he saw a butterfly or something and went after it with his camera," Fitch said. We all laughed. Dillon was easily distracted by anything that was alive and not human. Most of his pictures were blurry or the animal was so far away you couldn't tell what it was.

"And this here's a raccoon," Dillon'd say, pointing to a dark spot in the picture. "See his striped tail?" We'd say we did even if we didn't.

"I'll go over and get him." I turned to Mo. "Want to come?"

"Sure," she said. "Race ya. Readysetgo!" We both ran for the Woods' house.

My running wasn't steady, I was laughing so hard, but I touched the porch rail right before Mo did. "I beat!"

Mo laughed. "You had a head start, but I'll give you this one."

"Ha!" I said, knocking.

Dillon's father opened the door. "Hello, Mr. Wood," I said. "Is Dillon coming out?"

"Dillon's not feeling very well right now. I don't think he'll be out today."

I could see behind him into the house. Dillon was sitting in a kitchen chair. He was bent over the table with his face hidden in his arms. His back was heaving the way it does when you're crying real hard.

I swallowed, suddenly afraid. Then Mo said what I'd wanted to but couldn't.

"Is everything all right, Mr. Wood?"

He put his hand on her shoulder. "Yes, everything's all right. Sam is going on a trip." His voice was quiet and a little shaky. "We just need time to talk here, that's all. Go on now and play." He started to close the door, then opened it again. "Thank you, girls. You're good friends to Dillon."

Mo and I stood there looking at the closed door for a moment. I slipped my arm through hers and we started back toward the field.

"Where do you think he's going?" I asked on the way. "He can't be leaving for college yet. That won't start until next fall."

"Maybe he got a job somewhere else."

"Maybe," I said, but I worried it was something else.

After we told the gang about Sam and how upset Dillon was, nobody felt much like playing ball. Instead we all went home to see if anybody's parents knew what was going on. Papa wasn't there, but Mama was.

"Sam is going south to help with the civil rights movement," she told us, ironing one of Papa's shirts. "He wants to try to help change things for the better."

"But, Mama, aren't the protesters getting beat up and put in jail?" I asked. "Why would he want to go do that?"

"Because it's something he believes in, that's why. He's doing a brave thing." She set down the iron and turned it off.

"When's he leaving?" I asked.

"Tomorrow."

"How long's he gonna be down there?" Billie asked.

Mama sat down with us on the couch. "I don't know."

"Dillon was crying," I said.

"I know, honey." She hugged me. "It's going to be hard on him and Mr. Wood. They've only had Sam back from the

Navy a few months and he's leaving again." She took Billie's hand and looked at him. "But Sam has to make his own decisions now."

We went out to the back porch and sat on the swing. After a while the Clearys and the Sherman twins showed up. Billie and I were the only ones who knew about Sam. We told them what Mama had said.

"I guess that's what Sam was always over here talking about," Alice said.

"Guess so," was all I could say. For some reason I felt guilty. Like maybe Mama and Papa were partly to blame for Sam's leaving.

We sat there, in silence. Me and Billie and Mo on the swing, Luke and Alice squeezed in a lawn chair, and Fitch and Owen on the top porch step. I looked at the side of the house where Dillon often leaned. He liked to stay standing so he could look out for nature stuff and Old Hairy. It didn't feel right, him not being there.

I leaned my head against Mo's. "I wish Dillon'd come out."

"He's probably okay now," she said. "He's just embarrassed that we saw him crying."

"Probably," I said, but I wasn't so sure. If I was Dillon I'd be worried. What if there was trouble at a protest and something happened to Sam? Sam . . . who wasn't Lucky anymore.

Chapter 15

Dillon came to school the next day, but he didn't show up at the bus stop until the last minute.

"Hey, Dillon," everybody said when he got there. He just nodded. Nobody knew what to say at first. It was strange, not being able to talk to someone I'd known all my life. Finally, I couldn't stand it anymore and just said what was on my mind.

"We're sorry Sam is leaving."

Dillon nodded and seemed to relax. Everybody else did, too. We could tell he didn't want to talk about Sam so we didn't.

"So are we gonna play ball after school?" Alice asked. "And is *everybody* going to be there?" She looked sideways at Dillon.

He laughed a little and said, "Sure."

Sometimes Alice went too far, but sometimes she knew *just* how far to push.

Mr. Stanley was sitting at his desk when we walked into the room. Mo squeezed my hand before going to her seat.

Everybody clapped when he stood up to greet the class.

"Good morning and thank you," he said. "I'm sorry it took me so long to get back. I received good reports from Mrs. Davis and I'm proud of you all. I know it's not easy changing teachers in the middle of the year. And now that I'm back, I'm sure you will miss Mrs. Davis."

I looked down at the floor by the bookshelves where I'd found the pen. Not me. I wouldn't miss her. I was glad she was gone. I wouldn't have to look at her face and know that, even when she smiled at me, she thought I stole things.

"There are only a few weeks of school left, but I'm glad we can end the year together," Mr. Stanley said. "We're going to use some of this time looking at poetry."

A few kids groaned. We had done poems earlier in the year. We had to memorize one and stand in front of the class and recite it. I didn't mind. It was like acting, like when we played cowboys or Robin Hood. But most of the kids didn't like it.

Mr. Stanley opened a book, cleared his throat and started to read:

> *There was a young lady from Lynn,*
> *Who was so exceedingly thin,*

That when she essayed
To drink lemonade,
She slipped through the straw and fell in.

The whole class laughed. He read another one:

There was a young farmer of Leeds,
Who swallowed six packets of seeds.
It soon came to pass
He was covered with grass,
And he couldn't sit down for the weeds.

Everybody laughed again. I heard some kids say how great it was to have Mr. Stanley back.

"Does anyone know what this style of poem is called?" he asked.

A boy named Dave raised his hand. "Humorous?"

Mr. Stanley smiled. "Yes, they are that. But remember earlier in the year when we read poems that had different rhyming patterns? Some poems that are written in a particular pattern have a name."

Ivy raised her hand. "Is it a limerick?"

"Excellent, Ivy, yes, it's called a limerick."

Mo raised her hand. "Will you read some more?"

"Yes," he said. *"We're* going to read more. And then we'll talk about structure. And *then"*—he paused for a second— "I'll want each of you to write a limerick of your own to memorize and share with the class."

Some kids groaned again, but most seemed to like the idea. I did, even though I was a little nervous about whether I could write one.

Mr. Stanley handed the book of limericks to Blanche, who sat in the first desk. Everybody read one out loud and passed the book back to the next person. It was how we usually read things. Some of the poems were funnier than others, but everyone seemed to like them and was anxious to read.

When my turn came, I read:

> *There was an old man with a beard,*
> *Who said, "It is just as I feared!—*
> *Two owls and a hen,*
> *Four larks and a wren,*
> *Have all built their nests in my beard!"*

After the last person read, Mr. Stanley wrote a limerick on the blackboard and showed us how the rhyme works.

"As you can see, limericks are usually about a person from somewhere and something he does or doesn't, was or wasn't, and then some final result of this quality or action. Your limericks will be due . . ." He looked at the calendar. "Let's share them on the last day of school. It will be a nice way to end the year," he said. "In the meantime, we'll be reading more, and looking at their rhyme and meter. Does anyone have any questions?"

"Can we write more than one?" Ivy asked.

"Certainly, but you'll only recite one in class."

Clayton raised his hand. "Do they have to be funny?"

Mr. Stanley looked surprised, but said, "They usually are, but, no, they don't have to be funny, as long as you get the structure correct." He walked over to the dictionary shelves and touched my shoulder as he passed.

"Remember we have a rhyming dictionary, if anyone needs to use it," he said, pointing to a book on the shelf. "And I'm here to help."

Mr. Stanley passed out mimeographed copies of some limericks for us to take home, then he let us spend some time working on ours.

Later we labeled the different parts of speech in sentences. Nouns, verbs, adjectives, pronouns, adverbs, conjunctions. I usually didn't like grammar much. But today I loved it. I even loved long division. I loved everything about school now that Mr. Stanley was back.

Chapter 16

Everybody was quieter than usual at lunch. I unfolded the wax paper from my slice of cake. Mama didn't get much store-bought dessert, but she did buy Spanish bar cake sometimes. It was dark brown and spicy and not dry like some cakes. It was shaped like a brick and had a thin layer of white icing in the middle and on top but not on the sides. I loved it, but Mama always only gave us a thin slice. Mo looked at it with wide eyes. I broke a piece off for her. She'd done the same for me lots of times.

It was a pretty day and we were all just chewing and looking out the window like Dillon did on a regular basis.

"Did anybody talk to Callahan about my radiation suit?" Clayton asked.

Nobody had.

"I guess you decided to believe me then?"

"Maybe we decided that we don't care," Ivy said. She was always talking back to Clayton.

"Yeah," said Jane.

The rest of us kept eating our lunches, but I smiled to myself. Ivy was right. I didn't care about Clayton's radiation suit anymore. If there was a bomb, I'd stay right at school with Mo and everybody until Mama and Papa came for us. I remembered Mama's Superman face. I knew she and Papa would come.

"Well, there's something else I didn't tell you before," Clayton went on. Nobody said anything, so he kept talking and we just let him. "My dad built us a bomb shelter under our backyard. It cost three thousand dollars and is as big as our living room. It has a generator for electricity, a filter so we can have good air, five beds with sleeping bags, canned food and water, and a toilet and everything. We've got enough supplies to last a month. We even have a Geiger counter. That's one of those gadgets that tells whether there's radiation around or not."

He took a breath then kept going. "So if the Russians attack and I'm at home, all we have to do is walk out to the shelter, and if I'm here at school, all I'll have to do is put on my suit and ride home on my bike." He crossed his arms over his chest and sat back in his chair.

"Why do you need five beds? There's only you and your mom and dad," Ivy said.

"Just in case we want to let somebody else in," he said.

I was trying not to pay any attention to him, but I

couldn't help listening and I couldn't help being surprised. Would Clayton be willing to share?

Luke took off his glasses. "Like who?"

"I don't know, exactly. My dad will decide," Clayton said. "He says maybe a doctor or somebody important like that, somebody worth saving."

"If you were allowed to pick someone, who would you take?" Luke wanted to know.

"Well, I'd have to think about that," Clayton said real slowly. I could tell he liked the idea of having the power to save someone or not. He looked across the table. "Maybe I'd pick somebody like Judd here."

Judd never said much, but now he spoke. "My dad says if there's another big war and they start dropping atomic bombs, it won't be worth living afterward anyway. He says the best thing that could happen is for a bomb to land right on our heads so we won't even know what hit us."

Nobody seemed to know what to say about that. Then Billie said, "Maz."

Everybody looked at him, confused.

"If I was picking somebody to save, that's who it'd be. Bill Mazeroski."

"Think they'll still be playing after the bomb?" Luke asked, smiling.

"Are you kidding?" Billie said. "Baseball is forever. Besides, there won't be nothin' else left to do."

We all laughed and it turned into a game. It was times like this when I loved my brother most.

"I'd save President Kennedy," Mo said.

"Elvis," Alice said, pretending to faint.

"Mr. Lips and Hips," Owen sang, imitating Elvis's voice. He stood up and started swinging his hips.

Mo and I giggled.

"Lassie," Ivy said, and we all started whistling the theme song from the TV show.

Clayton looked mad. He didn't like us turning his bomb shelter into something funny.

"I'd save Reverend Martin Luther King," Fitch said. "Our father says he's a good man."

"Yeah?" Clayton said. "Well, *my* dad says he's just a troublemaker and the people down South, colored and white, are getting hurt because of him. He might even be a Communist spy, turning people against their own government."

It got quiet again. With the news about Sam, this was not something any of us wanted to talk about. I glanced at Dillon.

"Clayton," he said, amazing us all. "You said if the Russians attack and you're home, all you have to do is walk out to your bomb shelter, and if you're at school, all you have to do is put on that suit of yours and ride home on your bike?"

Clayton nodded and said, "That's right." He looked real pleased to be back in the limelight.

"Well." Dillon stood up. "What if you're at the A & P supermarket?"

Clayton frowned, like he was thinking real hard.

"Come on, guys," Dillon said. "It's recess."

If I was old enough to be inclined toward romance, I'd have fallen in love with Dillon right there on the spot.

Chapter 17

"Oh, Lord," Mama said about something in the paper. Papa had already left for work, and Billie was still getting ready for school.

"What, Mama?" I asked, looking over her shoulder to see what she was "Oh, Lording" about.

She closed the paper. "Nothing for you to be concerned about," was all she said. It was one of those answers that didn't tell me anything.

I'd never been much interested in the TV news or the paper except for the funnies, but since Sam had gone, I found myself listening and reading more. Trying to, at least. But lately, when Walter Cronkite came on, Mama or Papa would find something for us to do. And now Mama was pretending there was "nothing to be concerned about" in the paper, when I was pretty sure there was.

I knew why. They didn't want us worrying about Sam,

and it's true that I *was* worried, at first. But after Sam left for Mississippi, I decided to keep a picture of that smile in my head, and I knew he'd be okay.

The phone rang and Mama went to answer it. While she was gone, I opened the paper. "National Guard Protects Negroes from Mob," the headline said. It was only a week after the bus burning. I held my breath a second, then saw that this was in Alabama again, not where Sam was. I was glad, but I understood why Mama was upset.

The article said that while the Reverend Dr. Martin Luther King, Jr. was speaking at a big church meeting, a mob of over five hundred people surrounded the building and started pushing cars over, breaking windows, and throwing fire bombs. The people inside were afraid the church might catch on fire. President Kennedy had to send in the National Guard and U.S. Marshals to get the mob to leave. Dr. King and the other people inside the church couldn't get out until four o'clock in the morning.

"Why didn't they want Reverend King to talk at that church meeting?" I asked Mama when she came back.

Mama sighed and sat down in a kitchen chair. "Because he is talking about change, and the people who are against him like things the way they are. Dr. King and other people want Negroes to have more rights."

"Like the Freedom Riders?"

"Yes, like them, and like Sam."

"Come on, Meg," Billie said. He grabbed his lunch and kissed Mama on the cheek.

I hugged Mama. She hugged me back real hard and said, "Go on to school now. Don't you be thinking too much on this, Meg."

"Yes, ma'am," I said.

And I tried not to. I just kept that picture of Sam's smile in my head.

Chapter 18

"Come on, Meg! Slam one!" Billie called from third base. He wanted me to hit him in real bad.

We'd been playing ball every day after school, and I was catching fine, but my hitting was way off. I was thinking too much, distracted by something. Mrs. Davis. It had been over two weeks since Mr. Stanley had come back, but, for some reason, the bad feeling was still inside me. And every time I got up to bat I found myself wishing Mrs. Davis was the ball and wanting to blast her right off the planet.

I tightened my grip and stepped closer to the plate. It was the bottom of the ninth, with two outs, and Luke's team leading 9 to 8. I had fouled twice, so already I had two strikes against me.

I took a deep breath and checked the field. Luke stood on the pitcher's mound with Fitch covering first and second, and Owen at third. Mo, their catcher, crouched behind me.

Alice was on first and Billie on third. There were only four players on each side, so there wasn't much coverage and it was easier to score when you got a hit. But you had to get a hit.

The pressure was on. Dillon stood on a log near home plate, saying quietly to himself, "Let her get a hit. Let her get a hit."

Mo punched her glove and yelled, "Come on, Luke, put it right here."

Owen kept chanting, "One more swing, we win this thing."

I choked up a little on the bat like Billie'd taught me. I concentrated on the ball, on slamming it like Billie said. I tried not to think about Mrs. Davis. Luke threw and I swung hard.

Crack! I made contact and the ball went flying, but something didn't feel right. I started to run toward first, dropping the bat as I went. That's when I realized what had happened. The bat, the only one we had, was busted. I stood there looking at it for a second.

"Run, Meg!" I heard Billie yell.

The ball had been fair.

I started to run, but it was too late. Luke tagged me out just as Billie slid into home.

"Phooey!" I said.

Billie got up and brushed himself off. "Shoot!" Then he saw the bat. "Aw, man!"

♦ ♦ ♦

"Boy, Meg, even Owen played better'n you today," Billie said later on the porch.

Owen grinned. I couldn't help smiling a little. At least I'd made *somebody's* day.

"Ah, leave her alone," Luke said. "Even Clemente gets into a slump once in a while."

"Easy for you to say," Alice grumped. "You guys won! Dillon would have hit us in."

Dillon just smiled. Sam had been gone nearly three weeks, and Dillon seemed to be getting back to his normal self again. I was sorry it hadn't been his turn.

"And now we can't even play again, till we get another bat." Alice folded her arms and looked at me.

"Wasn't Meg's fault," Billie said. "That old bat must have been ready to go." I'd never understand brothers. One minute they're criticizing you and the next they're sticking up for you.

"Yeah, Alice," Mo said. "You were up right before Meg. The bat might have started cracking then."

Alice grinned. "I guess. Sorry, Meg."

Mama came to the screen door. "Dillon, your father called. He wants you home. Billie. Meg. It's about time you came in, too."

My stomach tightened. Something was wrong. I could tell by Mama's voice.

"Yes, ma'am," we said.

"See you," I said, and we went inside while everybody else scattered.

Papa was sitting in the living room. His forehead was creased in a frown. I sat next to Billie on the couch and Mama sat next to me.

Papa took a deep breath. "I don't know that we should be worried, at this point, but . . ." he paused, "Sam is missing."

"What?" I said. Billie put his hand on my arm. It was a signal to let Papa talk.

"When Mr. Wood called Sam's hotel in Mississippi he was told that Sam had checked in, but that no one had seen him or the car he was driving for the past two days. That was yesterday. Today a man from the NAACP phoned Mr. Wood. He said Sam was supposed to attend a meeting two nights ago, but he never showed up."

I started crying. Dillon. All I could think of was Dillon. Mama held me.

"We wouldn't be telling you this now, but we want you to be able to help Dillon as best you can," Papa explained. "The only way to do that is to know the situation."

"What do you think happened?" Billie asked. He had moved over to sit on the rug by Papa's chair. All I could do was hug Mama.

"We don't know," Mama said, her cheek against my forehead. "But Sam is smart. We just have to believe he's all right."

I looked up and studied her face, but I didn't see what I'd hoped for. There was no Lone Ranger, no Superman this time.

Chapter 19

I couldn't go to sleep that night. I wondered if Billie was awake, too. The moon was shining in the window so I could see that he was facing the wall.

"Billie?"

"What?"

"Do you think Sam is dead?"

"Don't you even say that!" Billie said, almost yelling. "Just go to sleep, Meg."

I started bawling again. I couldn't help it.

Billie put his pillow over his head for a few minutes, then he came over to my bed and sat down.

"I'm sorry, Meg. I'm sorry." He was crying, too.

We hugged. "It's just like Mama said," he told me. "Sam's okay. He was in the Navy, remember? He can handle things."

I wanted to believe him, but I remembered the look on

Mama's face. I just knew something bad had happened to Sam.

In church the next morning, I prayed real hard. I prayed for Sam and I prayed for Dillon and I prayed for Mr. Wood. I prayed that all of us would have Sam back safe again in Mayfield where he belonged. In Mayfield, where we'd play ball and build snow forts. But it didn't do any good.

When we got home Mr. Wood came over. I wasn't finished changing out of my Sunday clothes, but I ran in the kitchen anyway, and I stood there in my slip while Mr. Wood told us how they had found Sam's car. With him inside. Dead.

The car was smashed into a tree by a dirt road. The police said it was an accident, but one of the people who had been working with Sam said the back and side of the car were dented, like another car had hit Sam's, like someone had run him off the road.

"Where's Dillon?" I wanted to know. No tears came this time. I'd cried myself out the night before.

"He's home . . . having a real hard time. We both . . ." He covered his face with his hand. "I gotta get back," he said. Papa put his hand on Mr. Wood's shoulder and they walked outside.

"I wanna see Dillon," I said, and ran for the door, but Mama caught me.

"We need to give Dillon some time with his father. Mr. Wood will let us know when."

I hung my head and went to put my play clothes on. I could tell Billie wanted to be alone, so I let him be. But I needed to do something. I couldn't stand just sitting around knowing.

When I opened the door to go out, Mama gave me *the look*. I knew she was thinking that *I* might be thinking of going over to Dillon's anyway.

"I'm just going out to work on the village," I said, which was the truth.

The village was in pretty good shape today. The anthill was a little bigger, but not busy like before. It was as if the news about Sam had reached the ants, and they were too sad to work.

I looked around for something new to add. I found an empty tin can by the trash. Maybe I could use that for something. I went to the garage and got the digging tool Mama used to plant flowers. Then I looked at the village. What did it need? There was a post office, a drug store, and a five-and-ten. There was a school and a gas station. There was even a Dairy Queen. It reminded me of Mayfield, and in that instant I knew that what we'd been building all these years wasn't just any village. It was Mayfield Crossing. Even the houses were set up in the same order as they really were—ours and Clearys' and Shermans' and Woods'.

I wanted to build a big roof over it. I didn't want any more floods or earthquakes. Mayfield needed protection. But I couldn't build a roof. All I had was a tin can.

I dug out a spot near all of our houses and placed the tin can on its side in the hole. Then I covered the open end with a flat rock, and was burying all of it except where the rock was, when Billie came out.

"What's that?" he asked.

"A bomb shelter," I said, "in case the Russians attack." I moved the rock from the opening. "See. This is how the people get in."

"Where are the Russians?" Billie asked, like it was a challenge.

In geography Mr. Stanley had shown us which direction the Soviet Union was from America. I marched over to a spot to the right side and a little above the village. "Over here." I picked up a stick and drew a shape in the dirt. Then I put my hands on my hips, a little bit mad, and said, "Don't you care about the Russians?"

Billie shook his head. He looked tired, like a grown-up, and when he spoke he sounded that way, too.

"No, Meg, I don't care about the Russians." He picked up a stick and walked to a spot right below the village. "This is what I care about." He drew another shape in the dirt and pointed to it.

"What's that?" I asked.

"Mississippi."

He stood there looking at me, waiting for it to sink in.

My stomach turned over, and now I wanted the village back the way it was. I took my stick and scratched out Russia. I scratched out Mississippi. I dropped to my knees and ripped the bomb shelter out of the ground with Mama's tool. Tears rolled down my face. Billie knelt down and put his arm around me. I hadn't cried myself out after all.

Chapter 20

Later, Billie and I went over to the Clearys and after a while the Shermans came, too. We talked some, but mostly we just sat on the old railroad ties that Mr. Cleary had put in last summer to make Mrs. Cleary some flower beds.

Luke stabbed the ground with a stick. "What exactly was Sam doing that made them so mad?"

"Papa says he was helping colored people sign up to vote," Billie said.

Alice frowned. "Don't they already vote?"

"The law says they can," Fitch said, "but Daddy says white people down South make them scared to try because something might happen to them."

Mo looked at the ground. "Like with Sam."

"It ain't right," Alice said. She yanked some grass from the ground and threw it.

"I wonder how Dillon is," Owen said.

We all looked over at his house. When I thought of Dillon, I often thought of Old Hairy, too, since it was Dillon who always spotted him. "Here comes Old Hairy," he'd say. I wanted to change the subject anyway, so I said, "Haven't seen Old Hairy lately."

"You complaining?" Alice asked.

"Maybe he's on vacation," Mo said.

"Where would he go? Transylvania?" Luke said.

Everybody laughed at Luke's joke.

I was going to mention the pick and shovel, but I knew the kind of stuff they'd start dreaming up. I'd already imagined enough on my own, and Mama had forbidden us from spreading any more Old Hairy stories.

We never got to see Dillon that day, and I figured he wouldn't be coming to school the next, but he did. Mama told us later that Mr. Wood didn't want Dillon moping around with nothing to occupy his mind except Sam, so he made him go. Besides, Mr. Wood had funeral arrangements to make.

At the bus stop, I wanted to hug Dillon as hard as I could, but I just stood there tugging my pigtail. I felt real shy, like I was meeting somebody for the first time.

Some of the others punched him lightly on the arm or patted his back, saying, "Hey, Dillon."

He didn't say much, just nodded and smiled a little.

When the bus came, he sat in his usual seat with Alice, but didn't talk all the way to school. None of us did.

Every morning the whole school said the Pledge of Allegiance and sang "Oh, Say, Can You See," then we'd all sit down, bow our heads, and pray. Today, right after the song, Mr. Callahan said over the P.A. system: "On behalf of Parkview School I would like to express our condolences to Dillon Wood and his family at the tragic loss of Dillon's brother, Sam. Please include them in your prayers today."

I looked across the room at Mo. *How did Mr. Callahan know?* She looked puzzled, too.

I bowed my head, but I didn't feel much like praying. I was confused. Except for the snow day, it didn't seem like God had been paying much attention to me lately. Mama says that God doesn't necessarily answer your prayers the way you want Him to, but that He *does* listen and then does what is best. I didn't think I'd ever understand how letting Sam die was best.

I didn't pray for Sam or Dillon or Mr. Wood that day. *Tell me why,* was all I prayed.

At lunch, some kids came up to Dillon and said, "Sorry about your brother." I knew Mr. Callahan thought he was doing something nice when he made that announcement, but it didn't help Dillon. I could tell he was uncomfortable with everybody knowing. He'd just nod and say, "Thanks."

"We heard about it on the news," Clayton said. "My dad says that some people think your brother was murdered by the Ku Klux Klan. That it wasn't an accident."

I didn't know it had been on the news. It was probably how Mr. Callahan found out, or maybe Mr. Wood had told him.

Clayton was waiting for Dillon to say something.

"Is that true?" Clayton asked.

"Clayton," Ivy said, "maybe Dillon doesn't want to talk about it."

"Yeah," Jane said, chewing her chipped ham sandwich.

Clayton looked all mad and turned to Ivy. "I'm getting a little sick of you, Miss Perfect, and your little windup doll here . . . always talking for them Mayfielders. Can't they talk for themselves or do they need you"—he paused and looked at the rest of us—"to baby-sit them?"

It did seem like Ivy was always sticking up for us against Clayton. But nobody'd asked her to and the rest of us had learned that it was better not to argue with him. It only made things worse.

Nobody said anything, so Clayton kept talking. "Well, if I was you, Dillon, I'd be speakin' up for myself *and* my brother. I'd be mad that my brother got killed. What in the heck was he doing down there stirring things up anyway? He ain't even colored."

I wanted to tell Clayton to shut up, but Papa had warned us about letting Clayton get us into a fight. I looked at Billie. Little beads of sweat were popping out on his nose.

"I'll tell you why," Clayton went on. "It's from growing up with them. My dad says the more you hang around with certain kinds of people, the more you start thinkin' like 'em yourself. You get mixed up in their business and start gettin' all kinds of stupid ideas in your head like you owe them somethin'. Well, look where it got your brother. Dead!"

Billie couldn't stand it anymore. He started to get out of his seat. "Clayton, you—!" but Alice snapped and said what I was thinking.

"Just shut up, Clayton! Don't you have any feelings at all? Leave Dillon alone."

Clayton stuck his chin out. "And what are you gonna do if I don't?"

Before she could answer, Judd dropped the sandwich he was eating and said, "Lay off, Clayton."

Clayton stared across the table at Judd. The rest of us did, too. Judd never said anything against Clayton. They were best friends.

Clayton grabbed his lunch, got up, and left the table. He looked hurt, and if it had been anybody else, I might have felt sorry for him. Judd gathered his lunch, too. He followed Clayton and sat down with him at another table.

We all finished eating, not saying anything more about

101

RETA E KING LIBRARY
CHADRON STATE COLLEGE
CHADRON, NE 69337

Sam. Luke started talking about how the new baseball season was going and everybody seemed happy to go along.

Dillon didn't say one word. I studied him some, trying not to be too obvious. He'd always had that wide-eyed look, like he was expecting something exciting to happen . . . some wild animal to show up. I loved that about him. But today he looked like Billie had the day before at the village. Old.

CRITICAL: ... LIBRARY
CHADRON STATE COLLEGE
CHADRON, NE 69337

Chapter 21

After school we played hide 'n' seek. We hadn't played ball since the bat broke. Papa said he'd get us a new one, but that was before we heard the news about Sam. Papa'd been busy helping Mr. Wood with the arrangements.

I was "It." Everybody who'd been caught was sitting on our front porch steps waiting for me to find Dillon. He was the last one left. Dillon was good at hiding because he didn't really hide. He used camouflage like animals do. Sometimes we'd find him curled up next to a rock the same color as his shirt, or he'd be lying in some leaves and twigs on the ground, not covered up or anything, just lying there. I'd looked in some places like that already and was getting frustrated. Nobody else seemed to know where he was either because, if they did, they'd usually start saying, "You're cold," if I wasn't anywhere close, or "You're getting warmer," if Dillon was nearby.

I walked around the house and started to go by the back

porch when I happened to glance up. Dillon was sitting right there on the porch swing. "Found him!" I called to the others, then I ran up the steps. "That was real smart." I was laughing at first, but I stopped as soon as I saw the tears on his cheeks.

"Yeah, I'm real smart all right," he said, wiping his face. "If I'm so smart, what am I doing living in this stupid place?"

By now the others were coming around.

"Dillon . . . he . . ." I didn't need to finish. They all knew he was feeling bad about Sam.

Billie sat down and put his hand on Dillon's shoulder.

"Leave me alone!" Dillon shouted. He pulled away from Billie and stood up. "You and your mama and papa. Always talking to him about that race stuff. It's their fault he went down there. It's their fault Sam's dead." He ran down the steps toward home.

"Sam was doing what he thought was right, Dillon," Luke called after him.

Dillon froze in his tracks and looked up at us. "But who made him think it? And why did it have to be Sam? He ain't even colored." He turned around and walked toward home.

We all stood there watching him go.

"Dag!" Fitch said. "Owen, let's go."

Billie went into the house.

Mo came over and squeezed my hand. "Dillon didn't mean it. He's just upset about Sam."

"Yeah, Meg," Alice said. "Clayton got to him today, that's all."

I couldn't say anything. I felt like I'd been punched in the stomach. I hoped they were right, but I had wondered if Mama and Papa were partly to blame, so I could understand Dillon thinking it, too.

For the first time in my life, I thought I'd lost a friend in Mayfield. It was like somebody had dropped a bomb on the Crossing. And all I could think to do was duck and cover, so I ran inside and went to bed early.

I couldn't sleep. I sang the duck-and-cover song to myself over and over, but it didn't help. It seemed like only yesterday we were playing ball and our worst argument was over a bad call on a foul tip. At the same time it seemed like forever since we'd been that way.

Feeling sorry for myself got me thinking about Mrs. Davis and her pen. I wished there was a hospital that could open me up and take out the bad feeling, so I could start fresh. I knew there wasn't any place like that, and I pulled my covers up over my face because I felt like crying again.

"Meg, honey, why are you in bed?" It was Mama.

The minute she took me in her arms, the dam burst. I told her everything about Dillon, about what he said about her and Papa, and then I told her about the pen.

Chapter 22

Mama hugged me and listened. She didn't scold me for not telling her about Mrs. Davis sooner. She just said, "I can't wash away your bad feelings about this, Meg. I wish I could protect you from people like Mrs. Davis. It's the kind of thing Sam hoped to change." She rubbed my back. "I know you're angry, but don't let it make you hateful. She's not worth that."

I remembered how I imagined Mrs. Davis's face on our baseball, how I wanted to hit her real hard. I *had* hated her. And I remembered what Sam said about a person's state of mind.

The thought of Sam made me know I had to ask. "Mama, is Dillon right? Is it our fault Sam went to Mississippi?"

Mama brushed back my bangs. "I can't say that your father and I didn't influence Sam. It was his idea to go, but we didn't discourage him."

"Did you and Papa *want* him to go?"

"We were proud of him, honey."

She paused for a moment. Her eyes had tears in them. "I believe Sam would have done something eventually. He was just that way. Your father and I were probably an influence on him, and so were you and Billie, the Navy, and Frank Sherman. Sam never did get over Frank's death."

"What happened to Frank, Mama?"

"Now, Meg . . ."

"Please . . ."

"Frank died of pneumonia. You know that."

"But what about the night Old . . . Mr. Slater brought him home? Sam said Mr. Slater was an exceptional person. Why, Mama?"

She turned away a moment, then she looked back at me and began. "That night Frank wanted to attend a party just across the tracks. A girl he was sweet on was supposed to be there. But Sam didn't like the boy who was giving the party, so he refused to go. Frank went by himself even though Mr. and Mrs. Sherman had said he could go only if Sam went. They were drinking at the party and, at some point, there were words and several boys dragged Frank outside and hurt him."

"Hurt him? But why, Mama?"

"Because they wanted to let Frank know they took exception to a Negro dating a white girl."

I remembered the people at the lunch counters, the people on the bus that was set on fire, the people trapped inside the church.

"How many boys were there, Mama?" My heart was pounding.

"Sam said five."

"Sam? But you said he didn't go?"

"He got worried about Frank and showed up later. After the fight was nearly over."

"Did Frank get beat up real bad?"

"Not as badly as he would have if Mr. Slater hadn't stepped in."

"Mr. Slater? How did he know . . . ?"

"I'll tell you something, Meg. Harry Slater has been watching over Mayfield since the day he arrived here. He followed Frank to the party. Frank rode there on his bike, but Mr. Slater walked, and by the time he got there it was dark and raining and the beating had already started."

The look on my face must have shown I was scared because Mama patted my hand.

"Frank got it bad, but those boys might have killed him right there if it wasn't for Mr. Slater. As soon as he got there and saw what was happening, Harry stepped in and put a stop to it."

"But there were five of them."

"You know how you kids always talk about what Mr. Slater carries in his knapsack?"

I nodded, my eyes wide. "Did he kill them?" I whispered.

"For heaven's sake, no," Mama said. "By now, Sam had arrived and he saw the whole thing. Mr. Slater pulled that hatchet out of his bag, held it up and said, 'Any of you lay another hand on that child, I'll take that hand right off!' "

"Old Hairy said that?"

Mama smiled and nodded her head.

"It was enough to scare them off, and Mr. Slater carried Frank all the way home. Sam said he tried to help, but Mr. Slater wouldn't let him, so Sam walked alongside pushing Frank's bike in the pouring rain.

"You know the rest of the story. They took Frank to the hospital. He had a couple of broken ribs and was pretty beaten up. It turned out that he had a punctured lung and came down with pneumonia. It was the pneumonia that killed him, but . . ."

"Sam . . ." I said.

Mama nodded. "Sam blamed himself for not going with Frank in the first place."

"Is that why he went to Mississippi?"

"I think it must have played a part, Meg. He wanted to do something to help people."

Suddenly the room felt cold, like winter. "Mama?" I was afraid to ask, but I had to. "Will Papa blame himself? Will he go, too?"

Mama held my face in her hands. "No, honey, your papa

is staying right here with us. I promise." She brushed my bangs back again. "Do you believe me?"

I studied her face. Her eyes were wet, but they looked sure and determined. Like Superman. I nodded and hugged her around her neck.

Billie and Papa came to the door. It was our real bedtime. "Are we interrupting something?" Papa asked.

"No," Mama said, tucking me in bed. "We just finished our talk."

After we turned out the lights, I couldn't stop thinking about Sam and Frank and Old Hairy. I was feeling kindly toward Mr. Slater, and not just because of what he did for Frank. I realized that Old Harry and I had something in common. It made me feel better, but my stomach hurt when I realized that I was a little bit like Mrs. Davis, too.

Just because I returned the pen didn't mean I stole it, any more than Old Hairy carrying a hatchet meant he used it for something bad. Just because he carried him home that night didn't mean he did Frank any harm. And just because Old Hairy was carrying a pick and shovel didn't mean . . .

"Billie?" I said. I knew he was awake.

"Huh?"

"Have you seen Mr. Slater?"

"No." He rolled over and propped his head on his hand. "Why?"

"Don't you think it's weird that he hasn't been around?"

110

"I guess."

I took a deep breath. I didn't know if Billie would understand, but I needed to do something for Mr. Slater. Mama said he'd been watching over us all these years, maybe he needed somebody to watch over him, too.

"I think we should go find him. Maybe something happened to him and nobody knows. Maybe he needs help."

Billie started laughing. "You're nuts, Meg!"

"No, really," I said. "He lives all by himself in the woods. Who would know if he was sick or something?"

"Maybe." Billie lay back. I didn't say anything. I could tell he was thinking.

"It might be fun," he finally said, "like an expedition."

I hadn't thought about it that way at all. I was just plain worried. But if making it into an expedition got Billie to agree, I wasn't going to argue.

"We'll get the Clearys and Fitch and Owen tomorrow," he said, rolling to his side.

"What about Dillon?"

He didn't answer right away. "We can ask," he said after a while, "but I don't think he'll come."

I punched my pillow. I wasn't sure the others would agree either, but I knew Billie was right about Dillon. It would be the first time we did something like this without him, and I wondered if he would ever be part of the gang again.

Chapter 23

Convincing the others to go looking for Old Hairy wasn't easy. I knew Dillon wouldn't come, but Owen and Alice were holding out, too.

"I think you've got things mixed up here," Owen said. " 'Werewolf comes, we run,' is the way it's done."

Fitch laughed.

"Yeah." Alice put her hands on her hips. "What if we find him and he's mad that we did? What if he pulls his hatchet on us?"

We'd had this conversation before. Ever since Sam and Frank had told us about finding the cabin, we'd all wanted to get a look at Old Hairy's place. But the thoughts of that bloody hatchet always gave us a reason not to go.

"Come on," Luke said. "It'll be fun. Besides . . ." He took off his glasses like he always did when he was trying to convince you of something. "The rest of us are going, even if you aren't. And if we *do* run into trouble, we'll need all the help we can get."

Alice folded her arms like her mind was made up. But I could tell by the look on her face that she was weakening.

"Okay!" she said. "But Mom's not going to like this." It was an excuse, like always.

"We just want to check on Mr. Slater," I said. "How could she be mad about that?"

"Meg's right," Luke said, putting his glasses back on. "Let's go."

Nobody argued with him. We put on boots and jackets and took knapsacks like we were going on a real expedition. We got long sticks for hiking and to beat a path if we needed to. Billie and Luke led the way.

I thought it would be spooky once we got into the woods, but it wasn't. It was quiet, and the farther we went, the quieter it got. Here and there beams of sunlight peeked through. We were careful not to make noise, so we saw chippies and rabbits and even a fox before it saw us and ran off. This was what Dillon had always tried to tell us about. I got a lump in my throat just thinking about him.

"Anybody else smell smoke?" Billie whispered.

I did. It was wood burning and it smelled good.

"There it is," Luke said, pointing ahead. It was a little

house made of logs with some smoke curling out of the chimney.

We all stood there looking at Old Hairy's cabin. I'm not sure what we'd expected, something from a horror movie maybe with barbed wire and old junk all around.

"It's kinda cool!" Mo said.

The windows were framed with wood shutters and you could see red and white checked curtains through the glass. The area around the house was neat and trimmed and there was a stone wall about waist high that surrounded the whole place, except for an open spot where you went in. There was a path made of stones that started at the opening and ended at the door. As we took slow steps down the path, I saw a garden on one side of the cabin. Near the garden was a pump.

"Look," I whispered. It was only May and things hadn't grown very high, but I could see straight rows of young plants coming up. Squirrels scurried everywhere, and it didn't take long to figure out why. Beside the front door was a big basket full of walnuts still in the shells and another filled with pine cones. Sometimes Mama bought walnuts, wreaths made from pine cones, or other homemade stuff from Old Hairy.

Mo pushed Luke's arm. "Look in the window."

"Why don't *you* look in the window," he said, pushing back.

"*I* will," I said.

Billie shrugged an okay and we walked over to a window at the front of the house. It was too high from the ground to see in, so Billie locked his hands together, I put my foot in, and Luke gave me a little boost up. Then he held my back to keep me from falling.

The inside was small and there wasn't much furniture, but it was neat and clean, just like the outside. The kitchen, which I couldn't see too well, took up half of the room, and the other half was the living room with a chair, a table that looked homemade, and a fireplace. Wood burned in the fireplace. A door off the living room probably led to a bedroom.

"Can you see him?" Fitch asked in a whisper.

"If he's in there, I'm outta here," Owen said, only he said "hair."

"No," I said, "but if he's sick he might be lying down, and I can't see the bed from here."

Luke helped me down.

"What's it like?" Mo asked.

"Did you see his hatchet?" Alice's eyes were wide.

"No."

"Are there spiderwebs and stuff?"

"No, Alice. It just looks like a normal place, clean and everything. Like a frontier cabin."

She frowned. "Maybe he has a cleaning lady."

The rest of us started to giggle.

"Be quiet!" Billie said, but he was smiling, too.

"Maybe he *is* a cleaning lady," Luke said.

We laughed louder.

"Shhh!" Billie said, trying not to laugh.

Everybody got quieter and Alice said, "I wanna see."

"Me, too," Billie said. "I didn't come all this way for nothing."

I was starting to feel like we shouldn't be there. I could see Mama's face and hear her saying something about respecting Mr. Slater's privacy. But I'd started this . . .

"I'm going around back to see if he's in the bedroom," I said.

Billie grabbed my arm. "No, Meg. Stick with me. We should all stay together." He was right. In the movies something bad always happened when people split up.

"But shouldn't we check to see if he's home before everybody starts looking?" I asked.

"Right, Meg. Let's all go," Billie said, taking charge.

This wasn't as high off the ground, so Billie and Luke could stand on tiptoes and see.

"Is he in there?" I asked.

"No," Billie whispered. "There's a bed, but he's not in it."

I turned away from the cabin and looked toward the woods. Old Hairy might show up any second, and Dillon wasn't there to spot him. I wasn't scared of him like I used to be, but he might not like us snooping.

My eyes followed the little stone wall to another break. This one opened to a path that led to what looked like an outhouse, which wasn't unusual for someone living out in the woods. I was about to turn back toward the others when I spotted an old wheelbarrow filled with sand near the end of the garden, and something else, something on the ground.

"Look, Mo," I said. We walked over to some big sheets of plywood.

We called the others and together we lifted a piece. Underneath was a deep square hole, as big as a room, with a concrete floor and cinder-block sides. I remembered Old Hairy with the pick and shovel.

"What is it?" Mo pulled a twig from her hair. "Is he building another house?"

"Sort of." I'd never seen one, but I knew exactly what it was. Old Hairy was making a bomb shelter.

Chapter 24

We never saw Old Hairy but figured he must be around because the fire hadn't been left for long.

"He's all right. He's just been too busy with the shelter to be coming around bothering us," Billie said on the way back.

"I guess Old Hairy plans to be terrorizin' the world even after the bomb," Luke said. Everybody laughed. I did, too, but it bothered me a little that Luke was talking like there definitely *was* going to be a bomb.

"Where would you guys go if there was a bomb and we were all at home in Mayfield?" I asked.

Alice knocked some mud off her boot. "Mom and Dad say we'd go down to the fruit cellar."

"Us, too," said Fitch.

Luke looked at Billie and me. "What about you?"

I'd never asked, but Billie must have because he said, "Yeah, we'd go in the cellar."

"Is that the same as having a real shelter like Old Hairy or Clayton?" I asked.

"Probably not," Billie said, "but we'd be okay." He put his arm around my shoulder as we walked out of the woods. "Think of all the junk we'd have to play with."

"I agree with Judd," Fitch said. "I don't think it'll matter what kind of shelter you have if there really is an atomic war. Everybody'll probably die anyway."

"Drop the bomb and we're all gone."

"Some people will live to start things over," Mo said. "Like with Noah and the Flood."

"Maybe," Fitch said, "but they'll probably be in the middle of the Amazon jungle. And would you want to be one of them?"

It was something to think about. If Mama and Papa and Billie were with me, it might be all right. But even that would be lonely if there was nobody else.

When we got back, everybody went on home. It was suppertime and some of us still had homework to do.

I wanted to talk to Mama about Old Hairy and the shelter, but I wasn't sure how she'd feel about us snooping around Mr. Slater's house. After supper, I just followed Billie to our room.

The last day of school was the day after tomorrow and our limericks would be due. Mo had written hers and had a real good one, a funny one to recite. I wanted mine to be funny, too, but my mind hadn't been working that way. I read what I'd written the day before:

> *A gallant young hero named Sam*
> *Liked to rescue good people from jams,*
> *So he went off to war,*
> *Then gave even more,*
> *'Cause his heart was as pure as a lamb's.*

It had the right beats and it rhymed like a limerick is supposed to. Mr. Stanley said they didn't have to be funny, but I didn't want to recite this one to the class. I looked out the window toward the woods where Old Hairy lived. Then I started a new poem:

> *Noah*
> *There once was a man named* ~~Hairy~~ . . .

Chapter 25

Dillon didn't come to school the last day because of Sam's funeral. Before going to the bus stop, I gave Mama my limerick about Sam and asked her to give it to Dillon. And I said a prayer for Dillon and Mr. Wood and Sam during our moment of silence, hoping God's schedule wasn't too full that day.

"Does anyone volunteer to be first?" Mr. Stanley asked the class. Sometimes people wanted to get it over with. If nobody volunteered, Mr. Stanley would start calling on kids. I had finished my limerick and felt okay about it, especially after I showed it to Mo and she laughed. I'd recited it to Mama and Papa the night before and they'd liked it, too.

Mo and I had agreed to get ours over with. I looked at her and we raised our hands.

"I'll go first, Mr. Stanley," Clayton whispered in a mocking voice behind me. "I'll shine your shoes, Mr. Stanley."

I knew he'd like to see me mad, so I pretended not to hear. Ivy glanced at Clayton, then tore a page out of her notebook and folded it up.

"All right, Maureen," Mr. Stanley said. "Why don't you recite, and Meg, you can follow."

Mo walked to the front of the room and handed her written poem to Mr. Stanley. Then she turned to the class and said:

> *A lady from Kalamazoo*
> *Thought she wanted to live in a zoo,*
> *So she wore her fur coat*
> *And behaved like a goat,*
> *Now she's in an asylum for looloos.*

Everybody laughed, even Clayton. Mr. Stanley started clapping and the whole class joined in. It was my turn. I didn't think mine was as good as Mo's, but when I saw the grin on her face, I didn't care.

> *Old Noah was building a boat*
> *To save elephants, monkeys, and goats,*
> *But with all of those twos*
> *And other stuff, too,*
> *He feared it might not even float.*

The class laughed and clapped again. I felt good, glad it was over. When I sat down, Clayton pulled my pigtail, but I just let it go.

After that, other kids wanted to recite. There were lots of good ones. Some people didn't get the beats quite right and sometimes they made words rhyme that didn't really rhyme like "man" and "ten," but everybody had one.

Ivy recited:

> *A man owned a bakery store,*
> *And each day he ate more and more,*
> *Until one day he found*
> *He'd gotten so round*
> *That he couldn't fit through the front door.*

Clayton was one of the last ones to go. Mr. Stanley had to call on him and a couple of other kids who wouldn't volunteer. When Clayton was walking up the aisle, I saw Ivy drop her pencil and, as she was picking it up, slip the folded paper onto his desk. I think she thought nobody saw her.

Clayton strolled to the front of the class and dropped his paper on Mr. Stanley's desk. Then he turned to the class, smiled, and said:

> *There once was a man who was Russian.*
> *He always looked like he was blushin'.*
> *The real reason why*
> *Was 'cause he was a spy,*
> *And off with our secrets he's rushin'.*

Most of the the class laughed, but it was a nervous kind of laugh, like nobody was sure it was supposed to be funny.

I thought it was clever the way Clayton had dropped the "gs" in "blushing" and "rushing" to rhyme with "Russian."

"Well," Mr. Stanley said, "Clayton has given us a lesson in civil defense *and* some creative word play. Does anyone remember what we call words like these?" He wrote "Russian" and "rushin" on the board.

I knew. They were homonyms—words that sound exactly the same but mean different things. We had talked about them earlier in the year.

Ivy raised her hand. "Homonyms."

Jane turned around and looked at Clayton. Ever since he'd called her a windup doll, she'd been mad at him. She raised her hand. "But isn't that cheating?" she asked. " 'Rushin' and 'blushin' aren't really words."

"You might say that," Mr. Stanley said. "What do other people think?"

I raised my hand.

"Meg?"

"Aren't you *allowed* to cheat a little in poems? I like what Clayton did."

"Yes," Mr. Stanley said. "There's something called poetic license that allows some rule breaking in poetry and other forms of creative prose. Mo did the same thing when she made up the word 'looloos.' "

Some kids laughed again.

"And I agree with you, Meg," Mr. Stanley went on.

"Clayton's 'cheating,' if you want to call it that, is what makes his limerick appealing. Good job, Clayton."

I knew Jane wouldn't like that I disagreed with her, but I did like Clayton's limerick. And Mama always said that when people aren't nice to you, you should try to find a way to be nice to them. I didn't turn around, even though I wanted to look at Clayton to see if it had made a difference.

Jane made a face at me at lunch and wouldn't sit down at first.

"Don't be that way," Ivy said to her. "Meg was just giving her opinion."

I looked up at Jane and smiled.

She looked at me and stuck out her tongue. Then she sat down.

I wanted to ask Ivy about the note to Clayton, but wasn't sure I should. It might be something private. It turned out I didn't have to because Jane whispered, "What was in that note you gave Clayton?"

Ivy smiled and shrugged, like it was no big deal. "Just a limerick."

Mo had heard, too, and the three of us looked at Ivy. She knew she was on the spot, so she reached in her pocket and pulled out a piece of paper. "Here's a copy," she said, laying it on the table for us all to see.

There's a person I know in this class,
Who thinks he has so much pizzazz,
But he better think twice
And start being nice,
Or he'll lose the few friends that he has.

Jane giggled, but I don't think Ivy meant it to be funny. I looked over at Clayton and Judd, sitting together at another table. Clayton turned and looked at us, but I couldn't read his face.

We had early dismissal, so after lunch we didn't do much. Mr. Stanley put our report cards in envelopes and handed back our limericks while we finished cleaning out our desks. Clayton didn't pull my hair or say any smart-aleck stuff to me the whole time. But when it was time to go home, I opened my desk for the last time, to make extra sure it was empty, and found a note:

I OWE YOU 1

There was no name or anything, but I knew it was from Clayton. I recognized his perfect handwriting.

Chapter 26

When Billie and I got home, we went on over to Dillon's. Mama had told us that she and Papa would probably stay over there for a while after the funeral.

I braced myself as we walked toward the house. I wanted to see Dillon more than anything, but I wasn't sure he'd want to see us. Billie knocked on the Woods' door and Mama let us in. The house was full of people. Mr. and Mrs. Cleary, Mr. and Mrs. Sherman, and a lot of people I didn't know. Mama said some of them went to church with the Woods. There were a couple of guys in military uniforms and some men in suits, who I found out later were from the NAACP.

"Hi," Billie said, as Dillon approached us. You could tell he'd been crying, but he seemed glad to see us. I walked right over and gave him the hug I'd been saving for days.

"Come on," he said, and we followed him into his bedroom.

Dillon had photographs taped all over his walls. Most were of animals, and there were some of trees and flowers. But there were pictures of Dillon, his dad, Sam, and even some of the gang, too. I'd seen most of them before, but he was always adding new ones. The pictures he'd taken with his new camera were bigger so they stood out. One that was stuck to his mirror made my breath catch. It was slightly blurry, like a lot of his pictures, but it didn't matter. Dillon had saved something that none of us would ever see again. Sam's smile. I swallowed to keep from crying.

We sat down on Dillon's bed. "What I said the other day, I . . ." His eyes were filling up and so were ours. "I didn't mean . . ."

"It's okay, Dillon," Billie said.

"I want to show you something"—he wiped his face with his sleeve—"from Lucky."

Lucky? None of us had called him Lucky since the snow-ball battle.

Dillon opened a drawer, took out an envelope, and handed us the letter from inside. "This was in his suitcase."

Billie unfolded it and held it so I could read, too.

Dear Dad and Dillon,

I'm writing this just in case something happens. I'm not suggesting that it will, but things are strange here and I want to be realistic. There are things that I would regret not having the chance to say.

We've never been a family to talk much about love,
but that doesn't mean it hasn't been there. In case I
don't get another chance, I want to tell you now that
I love you both so much it hurts. And I am lucky.
Yes, you read right. I am Lucky, just like Mom
said.

Dillon, when I came home I said I didn't want to be
called Lucky anymore. I don't know what got into me.
Somehow being in the Navy made me see all the
ugliness in life and forget about all the good. I've done
a lot of thinking since I've been down here. Thinking
about how it is back there in Mayfield, how it was
before I left for the Navy, and how it was after I came
home for those good months. You know what? It was
the same as it always was, and I loved that, because
what's normal in Mayfield is a fairy tale most every
place else.

I wish we could put our little town in bottles and
send it all over the country, all over the world, so
everybody could have some. But we can't. And that's
why I'm down here. Maybe I'm kind of like one of
those bottles, here to spread some of the goodness of
Mayfield, some of what I was lucky enough to be born
to. I don't want to die, but when I do, I want my life to
have been worth something.

All my love,
Lucky

I couldn't talk. I'd been feeling so many different things lately my head was swimming

"He's a hero," Billie said, tears on his face.

Dillon smiled. "Dad is talking with some people who are trying to prove it wasn't an accident."

Billie and I nodded.

The three of us sat there not saying anything for a while. Even though Sam was gone, I was glad we could call him Lucky again. It was like something that was out of place got put back where it belonged.

The letter got me thinking. I'd been feeling like maybe it wasn't such a good thing that Mayfield was special. Maybe it just made it harder for Mayfielders to fit in other places like Parkview or the Navy. But Lucky's letter made me feel proud.

I looked at Dillon. He was in his Sunday suit, but his hair was such a mess you could hardly tell the cowlick from the rest. He was our friend and always would be.

Dillon touched my arm. "Thanks for the poem, Meg." He leaned over and kissed my cheek.

Nobody knew what to say after that, so Billie told Dillon about going to Old Hairy's cabin. Naturally, he wanted to go see it, too, especially after I told him how pretty the woods were. We decided to to go on Saturday

"I'll bring my camera," Dillon said.

Chapter 27

On Saturday, Billie and I did our chores and sat down to watch *The Roy Rogers Show.* We weren't meeting the gang until noon because the Clearys were clothes shopping for their Sunday school picnic.

We were both singing "Happy Trails" when someone came to the front door. Mama answered it, then she called Papa, and instead of inviting the person in, they both went out on the porch. Billie and I ran to the screen door and looked out.

A man was sitting on the glider with Papa, and Mama was in a chair. They were talking real quiet, so I couldn't hear everything they were saying, just some things like: "When are you leaving?" "Are you sure this is what you want to do?"

I looked at the man. He was wearing a blue sports coat and tie and there was a worn suitcase on the porch beside him. I studied his face. He had gray hair, cut short. His nose was a little bit freckled, but not as much as the Clearys'. There was something familiar about him, but I didn't think I knew him. Then I saw his eyes. They were a pretty green color.

I sucked in air. "Billie, it's . . ."

"I know," he said, as surprised as me.

It was Old Hairy. But he wasn't hairy anymore. He'd shaved all his whiskers off.

"Glory," I said, staring at Mr. Slater's new smooth face.

I stepped back when Papa came into the house and reached for the coffee can he used as a bank. He'd been saving for a washer for Mama. Papa went outside and handed some bills to Mr. Slater.

"It isn't much," Papa said, "but maybe it will help while you're there." He sat down. "I should be going with you."

"No, your place is here," Mr. Slater said. "You could look after my place while I'm gone, though."

"Be glad to," Papa said, nodding.

"And I'd be obliged if you'd cover over that hole I dug out for a root cellar. Never did get it done, and as it is, somebody could fall in and get hurt."

Root cellar?

"I'll get over there right after church tomorrow," Papa said.

Mr. Slater handed Papa a long box and said something

132

that I couldn't hear. Then they shook hands, and he picked up his suitcase and started toward the porch steps.

"Bye, Mr. Slater," I said as he passed the screen door.

He stooped down to my eye level. He was so close, I could see the creases at the corners of his eyes as he smiled at me and Billie.

"You kids take care of Mayfield while I'm gone," he said. His voice was deep, but nice.

He walked off the porch. Mama and Papa came inside.

"Mr. Slater is going away for a while," Papa said.

"Where's he going?" Billie and I asked at the same time.

"Mr. Slater is very upset about what happened to Sam," Papa explained. "He's talked with some of the people from the NAACP and he's going to help with the organization."

"Old Hairy?" Billie said. "What can *he* do?"

"First of all," Mama said, "I've told you before that Mr. Slater isn't any older than your father and me." She *had* told us that. His hair just went gray when he was young.

"Second, Mr. Slater is a resourceful man," Mama said. "He's had to be, living by his wits all alone in the woods. After the war, he chose to separate himself from the world outside of Mayfield. Sam's death made him decide to come back."

"What's that?" I asked.

"It's for you kids," Papa said, handing us the box.

We set it on the kitchen table and opened it. A baseball bat.

Billie turned it over in his hands. "Looks like he made it himself."

For a second, I wondered how he'd found out we needed one. But like Mama said, Old Hairy was always watching over us whether we knew it or not. I thought about how, even though he was always showing up and scaring us, he seemed to be around when we needed him, too. Like when we first started going to Parkview and he'd been there at just the right times, like the night he followed Frank.

I looked at the bat more closely. Carved in one side was: "Mayfield Slugger" then in smaller letters: "Old Hairy Model."

I laughed. "He must not have minded us calling him that."

"Come on, Meg," Billie said, holding up the bat and pulling me out the door. "Let's go see if anybody wants to play ball."

Billie shoved me when we got outside. "*Bomb* shelter," he said, shaking his head and smiling. "Meg, you have some imagination."

"*So,*" I said, pretending to pout. Then I laughed, and we ran toward the field. Everybody else was already there. We had a lot to tell them.

I thought about Old Hairy leaving his nice little house, leaving Mayfield. Maybe Old Hairy was like Lucky. Maybe he wanted his life to be worth something.

Lucky said people aren't always what they seem, and he was right about that. He also said that Mayfield hadn't changed, but I knew it had. He was gone. And Frank. And now Old Harry Slater was going, too.

I figured I'd be leaving the Crossing myself someday. But I knew that I was lucky to live here now, and that what was good about Mayfield would always stay with me.

A Note from the Author

When I was growing up in the 1950s and early 1960s, many people worried there would be war with Russia and that atomic bombs could be dropped on the United States. Schools conducted "duck-and-cover" drills as part of the federal Civil Defense program. I remember these drills and the "fallout shelter" signs posted on public buildings.

Some people built their own family-size bomb shelters using plans provided in Civil Defense manuals. These manuals also listed the equipment and supplies needed for the first fourteen days after an attack, when radioactive fallout was said to be highest. Like Clayton's family, those who could afford to spend several thousand dollars bought ready-made, self-contained underground shelters. These units came equipped with electric generators, air filtration systems, radiation detectors, protective suits, bunk beds and air mattresses, blankets, sophisticated radios, canned food and water, and other basic supplies.

By the mid-1960s, air-raid drills and shelters became less popular as we learned about the true nature of radiation and discovered that shelters would provide very little protection. More people talked about preventing a nuclear war than surviving one.

About 200,000 bomb shelters were built between 1950 and 1962. None was ever used for its intended purpose.

Some families closed their shelters permanently. Others converted shelters into wine cellars, storm cellars, mushroom gardens, teenagers' retreats, playhouses for kids, or even extra bedrooms for unpopular guests.